It's the summer of 1991 and serial killer Jeffrey Dahmer has been arrested. His monstrous crimes inspire dread around the globe. But not so much for Emory Hughes, a closeted young man in Chicago who sees in the cannibal killer a kindred spirit, someone who fights against the dark side of his own nature, as Emory does. He reaches out to Dahmer in prison via letters.

The letters become an escape—from Emory's mother dying from AIDS, from his uncaring sister, from his dead-end job in downtown Chicago, but most of all, from his own self-hatred.

Dahmer isn't Emory's only lifeline as he begins a tentative relationship with Tyler Kay. He falls for him and, just like Dahmer, wonders how he can get Tyler to *stay*. Emory's desire for love leads him to confront his own grip on reality. For Tyler, the threat of the mild-mannered Emory seems inconsequential, but not taking the threat seriously is at his own peril.

Can Emory discover the roots of his own madness before it's too late and he finds himself following in the footsteps of the man from Milwaukee?

THE MAN FROM MILWAUKEE

Rick R. Reed

A NineStar Press Publication

www.ninestarpress.com

The Man from Milwaukee

Printed in the USA

Print ISBN: 978-1-64890-045-7

First Edition, July, 2020

Also available in eBook, ISBN: 978-1-64890-044-0

Warning: This book contains sexually explicit content, which may only be suitable for mature readers, deceased family member, kidnapping, violence/gore, attempted murder, and death of a parent.

For those readers who've been with me since my horror beginnings—this one's for you.

He learned only in bits and pieces of that wonderful blossoming of dark and lovely flowers: one was revealed to me by a scrap of newspaper...

—Jean Genet, Our Lady of the Flowers

I had these obsessive desires and thoughts wanting to control them to—I don't know how to put it—possess them permanently.

—Jeffrey Dahmer

Monsters are real, and ghosts are real too. They live inside us, and sometimes, they win.

—Stephen King

PART ONE

Summer

Chapter One

HEADLINES

Dahmer appeared before you in a five o'clock edition, stubbled dumb countenance surrounded by the crispness of a white shirt with pale-blue stripes. His handsome face, multiplied by the presses, swept down upon Chicago and all of America, to the depths of the most out-of-the-way villages, in castles and cabins, revealing to the mirthless bourgeois that their daily lives are grazed by enchanting murderers, cunningly elevated to their sleep, which they will cross by some back stairway that has abetted them by not creaking. Beneath his picture burst the dawn of his crimes: details too horrific to be credible in a novel of horror: tales of cannibalism, sexual perversity, and agonizing death, all bespeaking his secret history and preparing his future glory.

Emory Hughes stared at the picture of Jeffrey Dahmer on the front page of the *Chicago Tribune*, the man in Milwaukee who had confessed to "drugging and strangling his victims, then dismembering them." The picture was grainy, showing a young man who looked timid and tired. Not someone you'd expect to be a serial killer.

Emory took in the details as the L swung around a bend: lank pale hair, looking dirty and as if someone had taken a comb to it just before the photograph was snapped, heavy eyelids, the smirk, as if Dahmer had no understanding of what was happening to him, blinded suddenly by notoriety, the stubble, at least three days old, growing on his face. Emory even noticed the way a small curl topped his shirt's white collar. The L twisted, suddenly a ride from Six Flags, and Emory almost dropped the newspaper, clutching for the metal pole to keep from falling. The train's dizzying pace, taking the curves too fast, made Emory's stomach churn.

Or was it the details of the story that were making the nausea in him grow and blossom? Details like how Dahmer had boiled some of his victim's skulls to preserve them...

Milwaukee Medical Examiner Jeffrey Jentzen said authorities had recovered five full skeletons from Dahmer's apartment and partial remains of six others. They'd discovered four severed heads in his kitchen. Emory read that the killer had also admitted to cannibalism.

"Sick, huh?" Emory jumped at a voice behind him. A pudgy man, face florid with sweat and heat, pressed close. The bulge of the man's stomach nudged against the small of Emory's back.

Emory hugged the newspaper to his chest, wishing there was somewhere else he could go. But the L at rush hour was crowded with commuters, moist from the heat, wearing identical expressions of boredom.

"Hard to believe some of the things that guy did." The man continued, undaunted by Emory's refusal to meet his eyes. "He's a queer. They all want to give the queers special privileges and act like there's nothing wrong with them. And then look what happens." The guy snorted. "Nothing wrong with them...right."

Emory wished the man would move away. The sour odor of the man's sweat mingled with cheap cologne, something like Old Spice.

Hadn't his father worn Old Spice?

Emory gripped the pole until his knuckles whitened, staring down at the newspaper he had found abandoned on a seat at the Belmont stop. *Maybe if he sees I'm reading, he'll shut up.* Every time the man spoke, his accent broad and twangy, his voice nasal, Emory felt like someone was raking a metal-toothed comb across the soft pink surface of his brain.

Neighbors had complained off and on for more than a year about a putrid stench from Dahmer's apartment. He told them his refrigerator was broken and meat in it had spoiled. Others reported hearing hand and power saws buzzing in the apartment at odd hours.

"Yeah, this guy Dahmer... You hear what he did to some of these guys?"

Emory turned at last. He was trembling, and the muscles in his jaw clenched and unclenched. He knew his voice was coming out high, and that because of this, the man might think *he* was queer, but he had to make him stop.

"Listen, sir, I really have no use for your opinions. I ask you now, very sincerely, to let me be so that I might finish reading my newspaper."

The guy sucked in some air. "Yeah, sure," he mumbled.

Emory looked down once more at the picture of Dahmer, trying to delve into the dots that made up the serial killer's eyes. Perhaps somewhere in the dark orbs, he could find evidence of madness. Perhaps the pixels would coalesce to explain the atrocities this bland-looking young man had perpetrated, the pain and suffering he'd caused.

To what end?

"Granville next. Granville will be the next stop." The voice, garbled and cloaked in static, alerted Emory that his stop was coming up.

As the train slowed, Emory let the newspaper, never really his own, slip from his fingers. The train stopped with a lurch, and Emory looked out at the familiar green sign reading Granville. With the back of his hand, he wiped the sweat from his brow and prepared to step off the train.

Then an image assailed him: Dahmer's face, lying on the brown, grimy floor of the L, being trampled.

Emory turned back, bumping into commuters who were trying to get off the train, and stooped to snatch the newspaper up from the gritty floor.

Tenderly, he brushed dirt from Dahmer's picture and stuck the newspaper under his arm.

*

Kenmore Avenue sagged under the weight of the humidity as Emory trudged home, white cotton shirt sticking to his back, face moist. At the end of the block, a Loyola University building stood sentinel—gray and solid against a wilted sky devoid of color, sucking in July's heat and moisture like a sponge.

Emory fitted his key into the lock of the redbrick high-rise he shared with his mother and sister, Mary Helen. Behind him, a car grumbled by, muffler dragging, transmission moaning. A group of four children, Hispanic complexions darkened even more by the sun, quarreled as one of them held a huge red ball under his arm protectively.

As always, the vestibule smelled of garlic and cooking cabbage, and as always, Emory wondered from which apartment these smells, grown stale over the years he and his family had lived in the building, had originally emanated.

In the mailbox was a booklet of coupons from Jewel, a Commonwealth Edison bill, and a newsletter from *Test Positive Aware*. Emory shoved the mail under his arm and headed up the creaking stairs to the third floor.

*

Mary Helen waited.

A cloud of blue cigarette smoke hung near the ceiling, ethereal. The smoke didn't cover the perfume Mary Helen wore, something called Passion. She had doused so much of it on herself that Emory wanted to cover his nose, to gag, to ask her if she was in her right mind.

But he said nothing, only smiled at his younger sister, who sat, long legs thrown over the arms of a brown corduroy recliner, staring dumbly at the screen. The flickering images of a sitcom made Mary Helen's face alternately light and then dark. Canned laughter erupted every few moments, and Emory prickled. He felt as though they were laughing at *him*.

He cleared his throat, hoping his sister would notice him. There was a time, not so long ago, when he, a fifteen-year-old boy, and she, a little towheaded girl of seven, would sprawl on the living room floor together, newspapers spread out in front of them, and share a box of powdered sugar doughnuts while watching TV together.

Those days were long past. Mary Helen had dropped out of high school in the spring and now seemed to have no occupation other than sitting around the apartment during the day and disappearing to God knows where at night, sometimes not returning until the early morning, when dawn's gray light worked its transformation on the apartment, giving the worn furniture and threadbare carpets definition and color.

"Hello, Mary Helen," Emory moved toward the TV screen. "What are you watching?" A little girl on the television was dramatically rolling her eyes as an older man explained the virtues of telling the truth.

Mary Helen shifted in her seat, put her feet on the floor. She grabbed the remote control from the end table beside her and banished the father and daughter to darkness.

"Nothin'." She lit another cigarette from the butt of the last. She blew a stream of smoke toward her brother.

Emory waved the smoke away. "Have you had anything to eat?"

She glared at him, pursing her lips together. "No. Have you?"

Emory put his briefcase on a spare chair in the dining room, loosened his tie. There was a fan blowing, and Emory stood in front of it. The fan delivered no relief; it merely blew the hot air around more intensely.

"How was Mother today?"

Mary Helen stood and examined a run in the back of her black stockings. "Shit," she whispered to herself, then looked up at her brother. She smiled and her eyes sparkled. For a moment, Emory smiled back, startled to see a return of the cheerful little girl who used to live here.

"Mother had a complete recovery today. In fact, she's not even in her room. She got up around ten, dressed herself in a pink linen dress—charming little chapeau with a veil, stockings, the whole nine yards. She then went down to the L station. Told me she was headed downtown, to fucking Marshall Fields, where she'd do a little shopping and have lunch in the Walnut Room. And then she was going over to Thirty Three Personnel on Dearborn to see if they had anything in her line…" Mary Helen took a deep drag on her cigarette and blew the smoke once more at her brother, shaking her head. "How the fuck do you think she is?"

Emory licked his lips and rubbed his hands together. His palms were sweating.

Mary Helen started toward the door. She wore a black miniskirt and a black leather vest under which was a sheer black-lace body shirt. She had dyed her hair platinum blonde and cut it so that it stood up in hard little spikes. She wore silver hoop earrings, rows of four in descending size, in each ear. Her nose sported a silver stud. Emory wondered what was to be pierced next but could never ask her. She had done her face up to make it paler than it already was and lined her eyes in thick black mascara.

"Did Mother eat anything today?" Emory called after her.

Mary Helen replied by closing the front door softly.

"Does Mother need anything?" he asked the closed door.

*

Emory paused, hand on the brass-plated doorknob to his mother's room, wishing he could have just one day when he wouldn't have to go inside. But who would take care of

Mother if he didn't? Mary Helen never went into their mother's room during the day, even though she was supposed to be at home to take care of her.

Emory wondered how smoking cigarettes and watching talk shows on TV all day qualified as caregiving, then chastised himself for thinking so unkindly of his younger sister.

Emory gripped the doorknob tighter and turned it slowly, wondering if this would be the day he'd open the door and find his mother dead. As he leaned on the door, letting his weight open it, he pictured her, glazed blue eyes staring up at the ceiling, body stiff and cold.

He despised himself for the thought that rushed forward—he'd be relieved. He paused for a moment at the entrance to his mother's room and noted how it was a shrine to both her dying and her life and the vitality that AIDS had drained from her. Her art was the only living thing in the room.

Back in the days before she was sick, Mother indulged her creative tendencies by taking pottery classes, and the room was a testament to her handiwork. She had talent, Emory had always thought. There was something ethereal about the small vases and whimsical figurines she crafted. They had a fairylike delicacy, enhanced by the bold colors Mother used to glaze them—cobalt blue, orange, crimson, chromium yellow, and black. Her masterwork, a gangly gargoyle, stood guard on the nightstand next to her bed, it's bloodshot aquamarine eyes staring away intruders. There was barely room for the figure, some twelve inches tall and heavy, on the table's top, crowded as it was with prescription bottles, water, and Mother's inhaler.

Emory sighed for all that had been lost so quickly and completely.

The room reeked of feces and urine, the odor hanging over it like Mary Helen's cigarette smoke in the living room. The smell rushed out, an assailant. Emory choked back a gag. The same scent greeted him every weekday upon his return home from work, and yet he never got used to it. It never failed to cause the bile to rise, burning the back of his throat.

Mother lay, head propped up on three pillows, staring vacantly ahead. If she noticed that Emory had come into the room, no sign registered in her eyes.

Mother was naked. Emory tenderly picked up the balled-up cotton nightgown at the foot of the bed, squeezing and releasing its soft, quilted nap with trembling fingers.

Perhaps if I just step back and quietly leave the room, she won't notice me standing here. Maybe if we just left her alone for a few days without care, she could let go, leave, and then she would be at peace.

And so would I.

Emory dropped the nightgown and bit the inside of his mouth hard enough to taste the copper of his own blood. The pain throbbed, and Emory explored the torn skin with his tongue.

Even now, after more than a year of taking care of her, Emory could barely stand the sight of her. Sometimes he tried to tell himself this thing on the bed was not really her. Her soul had departed long ago, perhaps when she was first diagnosed. He recalled coming to the clinic on Wilson Avenue with her that fateful day, reading an old issue of *Newsweek* as Mother went into an office with a counselor to get her results. They were both confident she had nothing to worry about, despite the night sweats and the low-grade fever.

Burned indelibly on his brain—the sight of the counselor opening the door to her office and Mother standing there, shaken, tears glistening in her eyes.

Now, maybe seeing his mother would be easier if she would stop deteriorating. Yet every day there was another lesion, purple and raised, eating her alive, faster and faster, insatiable in its hunger. Every day, Mother wasted away more; now her ribs were clearly defined; a skull grinned out beneath the stretched white skin of her face.

Illinois Masonic had an AIDS ward and they now admitted women, but Emory couldn't do that to the woman who had raised him, who had loved and nursed him through his own myriad illnesses.

"Who the hell are you?"

There it was—her voice. It was still her voice. That was the amazing thing. This thing still sounded like Mother...the same velvety voice, tinged still with the accent of her North Carolina girlhood. Emory could still recall that voice reading him the story of *The Poky Little Puppy* when he was a child.

"Why, Mother, it's your boy. Emory. You know that." Emory shook his head, grabbed a towel and started to sop up the mess under his mother.

"I don't have any kids! No boys! You asshole. I asked you who the hell you were, and you better think of something better than that before I call the police, young man!" Emory wondered where the strength came from that let her have such indignation as she wagged her finger at him.

He sighed. "Don't you remember, Mother? Emory? Mary Helen?" Emory touched her forehead, brushing away a strand of straw-like hair from her face. Her forehead was hot, fevered demons racing around, consuming what was left of her brain. His palm grazed a Kaposi's lesion. It was raised and crusty, making Emory recoil. He wiped the hand that had touched her on his khaki pants.

She grabbed that same hand and squeezed it. "I know who you are! You can't fool me. You're the one's been tryin' to steal my dreams. Yes! Just in here last night, trying to lift my dreams from my head!" Mother's stare was accusing, her eyes moist. "You just go on, go on and get out of here, you filthy pervert, before I call the cops."

Mother began to cry as Emory turned her gently on her side so he could slide the soiled bedding out from underneath her.

*

Later, Emory, alone in his room, turned his portable TV on. The ten o'clock news would be on in a few minutes, and Emory wanted to see what they had to say about Dahmer. While he waited, he pulled that day's newspaper from his desk, rereading the front-page story.

The picture of Dahmer drew his eyes away from the type. How could he have done it? What must have driven him? Why would he want to do such horrible things?

As he pondered these questions, a memory, completely unbidden, came to him, rising up like Technicolor pornography. No matter how hard Emory tried to concentrate on the newspaper or even the boys' voices outside his window, it kept coming back, almost as if it had a life of its own, telling Emory: I will not be denied.

Earlier that summer, another hot night, very much like this one, when the moisture in the air wed the heat and the two became an unstoppable force, omniscient in delivering energy-sapping misery to the minions—those who could not afford air-conditioning.

Howard Street, a dangerous place, filled with shouts and come-ons from prostitutes. How did Emory's walk along the lakeshore bring him here? It was as though his feet had minds of their own.

A siren's call: the adult bookstore across the street beckoned. Its tawdry blinking lights and fluorescent signs in the windows promised X-rated delights for a mere quarter.

Emory had sworn to himself he would never return there. Ever. He had made his resolve strong. Steeled himself to never go inside that sick place, where the worst diseases, ones dealing death, were freely exchanged in the dark shadows of filthy peep-show booths, the floors littered with dirt, cigarette ash, and discarded condoms. He had told himself that he would be a healthier person if he never went inside such a place again. Such places were beneath him.

Yet, he waited for a break in the traffic and dashed across the street. A hot wind blew his ash-blond hair off his forehead. Everyone was staring at him, and they all knew what was on his mind.

The door's metal handle was cool, and Emory, heart pounding, sweat oozing out of his pores, and his resolve shaken but not gone—*I'll go in, but just to see what it's like*—yanked the door open.

After giving the man behind the counter two dollars in exchange for a handful of tokens, Emory went to the back part of the store where the video booths were. A line of flashing lights lined the ceiling, doing little to combat the darkness, settled upon the room like fog. A few men, hands thrust in pockets or smoking cigarettes, milled about, pretending to read descriptions of the pornographic movies they might select in the booths, but Emory could see their quick glances at him out of the corners of their eyes.

Emory's stomach rolled, and he tried to keep his eyes cast downward. *All I'll do is look at a movie and then leave.* Emory ducked into the first booth he came to. Hands shaking and palms slick with sweat, he pumped several tokens into the box that would bring the video screen before him to life.

Feeling sick, but transfixed, Emory stared at the screen, where a young boy, sprawled across a table, was being fucked ruthlessly by an older man. His legs were thrown up, partially hiding the older man's hairy chest. The older man's cock was huge, sliding in and out of the boy's ass, and Emory wondered if the pain on the boy's face and in his whimpers was real.

Emory ignored the tightening in his pants, biting his lower lip hard enough to bring stinging tears to his eyes.

The door behind him squeaked, and Emory's spine stiffened at the warmth of someone else sliding into the booth. The shadow of the man fell across the wall. Emory didn't turn but stood mute as strong hands slid around his waist, encircling it. Emory said nothing, as moist lips, like slugs, crept across the back of his neck. Said nothing as the stranger's big fingers fumbled with the button and zipper of his jeans. Said nothing as he yanked Emory's jeans to his knees. Said nothing as clothes rustled behind him. Said nothing as the heat of a penis pressed against the crack of his ass.

The man growled in his ear, and Emory braced his hands on the wall before him as the man slicked his cock with spit and pushed into Emory's ass, not stopping until he broke through the ring of muscle.

Emory gasped, the pain sudden and intense—throbbing. White-hot needles.

Emory began to cry as the man thrust into him. He felt dizzy, nauseous, but gripped his knees anyway, bending over so that the man could enter him more deeply.

His own cock softened as the man's thrusts grew more rapid, harder, as if suddenly what this man wanted to be was a messenger of pain rather than pleasure.

"Never again," Emory whispered to himself over and over. "Never again."

Emory's head jerked up: the images of memory scattered at last, leaving him breathless and clawing his faded quilt. A pool of semen, viscous and warm, had pooled beneath him.

And in front of him, on the screen, was Jeffrey Dahmer, being led, handcuffed, into a courtroom. Dahmer wore the same blue-and-white striped shirt he wore in the newspaper's photograph.

The face on the screen was terrified. Emory was sure of it. He was also sure that the terror was born of feeling out of control. He knew Dahmer, he thought, and understood him. He couldn't help himself.

And at once, Emory felt he had a unique understanding of the killer. Empathy was probably a more apt word.

Tomorrow, he would find out the name of the prison where Dahmer was confined and Emory would write him and let him know there was at least one person who appreciated what he was going through, without judgment. Understood, really, that none of this was Dahmer's fault.

Chapter Two

Sunlight filtered in to Emory's room, and he groaned, pulling the pillow over his head. He preferred winter, when daylight came later in the morning and departed earlier in the afternoon. Darkness had always been a friend to him.

Because it was only six a.m., he had another hour in which he could sleep, but even snuggled down into the body-warmed bedding, he found that slumber elusive.

Sighing, he sat up and looked around the room. Across from his bed (maple headboard he'd had since he was a little boy) was his desk, also a relic from boyhood days, and on it, the *Trib* from yesterday with Jeffrey Dahmer's photo on the front.

He got up and glanced down at the grainy photo and next to it, the spiral-bound notebook he'd set out the night before to write to him. There was something in that face that kept drawing Emory back, and it chilled him that he was so inclined. But in those bland, blond features, something called out to Emory—a plea for understanding, maybe, or simply a need to connect with another human being.

Another human being like him?

He shivered. Emory pulled on a T-shirt, and in it, along with his plaid boxers, he came out of his room into the rest of the apartment.

It was quiet, save for the rumble of the L a couple of blocks over. The door to Mary Helen's room was shut, and he knew better than to knock, or worse, open that door. She probably wasn't even in there, anyway. Who knew where she went at night?

He stopped outside Mother's door, listening. All was still, so he turned the knob slowly and then opened the door quickly, hoping it wouldn't creak. The door complied, staying mute. Emory slipped inside her room and paused beside her bed. Mother's head stuck out from a mound of blankets, and for a moment, Emory could almost forget her sickness, her nearness to death. She slept and the slackness of her features lent her an innocence. There was even a little color in her wan cheeks, probably a result of how warm she must be in this sweatbox of a room, buried under blankets, fever stoked. There was a sour smell in the air that turned Emory's stomach, especially this early in the morning. He knew there'd be breakfast to make, even though she'd barely touch it, and cleaning up to do.

But, for now, she slept, and Emory knew that meant he'd have a few minutes, maybe even a half hour, to selfishly tend to himself. He closed his eyes and let a little sigh of relief escape his lips.

Back in his own room, he sat at his desk, picked up a Bic pen with the tip chewed, leaving it marred and coarse to the touch. He closed his eyes for a moment, the pen poised above the lined paper.

And then he began to write.

The words flowed out of him without thought, as though he'd composed what he said as he slept. And maybe he had because he could vaguely recall an image of Dahmer, standing over him as he slept, softly mouthing words he couldn't quite hear or understand. He might have even been singing.

*

Dear Mr. Dahmer,

You don't know me, although our paths might have crossed one night on one of your visits to Chicago. But I doubt that. I'm sure I'd remember if you and I had ever been in the same room.

I wanted to take a moment and write to let you know there's one person out here who understands what you're going through. I fight my own demons, day after day, and know that sometimes our best intentions get crushed under the weight of needs we have no way of understanding, let alone escaping, try as we might to be good.

I know.

I know what a horrible thing it can be to be compelled to do things you know are wrong, evil, but for whatever reason, you're built to be unable to resist these needs. I have them. To some degree, I suspect we all do. Yours are much worse than the average person, yes, but that doesn't mean you wanted to feel the things you felt. Things that drove you to do what the papers say you did...

Anyway, if you get this letter, I'd love to hear back from you. I know right now the whole country hates you and gazes at your face with horror. But

I don't. I see a young man like myself, confused and full of pain because he can't help being who he is.

We're both twisted. In different ways, but I do know what you're going through right now, believe it or not. I see you sitting in a cell, maybe relieved now that your hands have been tied, so to speak.

You can be good now.

I envy that, just a little bit.

I wish I could be good. I'll keep trying, but it seems like the harder I battle the demons inside, the more they persist.

Anyway, if you get this (I don't know how mail to prisoners works—I've never written to anyone in jail before), please take the time to consider me a friend you can talk to.

I'll be anxiously awaiting your response.

Very truly yours,
Emory Hughes

*

Emory let the pen drop to the notepad so he could rub his eyes. Suddenly, they burned as they did when he stayed up too late, his body starved for sleep. He groped around in the top left-hand drawer and brought out an envelope. He folded the letter and stuck it inside. When he licked the glue, he imagined he was kissing Dahmer and then forced the thought away, as if it were something foreign and not the product of his own lustful mind.

He addressed it:

Mr. Jeffrey Dahmer

Prison System

Wisconsin

USA

He hoped that would be good enough—after all, there was no more notorious killer in the country right now.

And then he picked up the pen again.

His fingers just about flew over the notebook paper of their own accord. The words, just right, continued to flow from Emory, using only instinct and no thought.

For the first time since he could remember, he smiled.

Chapter Three

Tyler Kay awoke, rolled over, and grabbed his tortoiseshell-framed glasses from the nightstand next to his twin bed. He lay awake, quiet, for a few moments, listening to the sounds of the world as it awakened. Birds chirped outside his window, which he insisted on keeping open in the summer, despite his parents' house having central air-conditioning. If his father ever caught him, he'd have a fit and accuse Tyler of trying to air-condition the "whole goddamn great outdoors." Downstairs, he could hear the kitchen radio, tuned to NPR, on the local public radio station and the murmur of his parents' voices in the breakfast nook.

His world was located in Wilmette, Illinois, on the same street he'd grown up on—Tenth, just north of Lake Avenue. His world was one of affluence, bright sunshine, a one-hundred-and-something-year-old white Dutch Colonial house with a gazebo in the backyard. His world encompassed an attorney father, a stay-at-home mother, two sisters, one two years older, and one five years younger. Both were still in school, the older at Northwestern in their MBA program and the younger still in high school at New Trier. He moved in an atmosphere of country clubs and weekends in Wisconsin at the family summer home—a coach house in Fontana, on the shores of Lake Geneva.

Tyler had just graduated from DePaul University in downtown Chicago with a Bachelor of Arts in English. Much to his dad's chagrin, Tyler longed to be a serious author one day, someone like Updike or Roth or Capote or Mailer—someone the world would hold in high esteem, a reliable mirror for our lives and our passions. His creative writing classes prompted him to write literary fiction, the kind of stuff he submitted to the *Atlantic Monthly* or the *New Yorker*, despite never having received so much as a form rejection from either publication. In the desk drawer opposite his bed were the pages of a half-written novel, inspired by Proust's *Swann's Way*.

And here it was—his first day at his first job out of college. Was he an editor at a newspaper or literary magazine? A book critic for the *Tribune* or *Sun Times* or even the *Reader*? Maybe he'd landed a job as an editor at Encyclopedia Britannica downtown? Surely, Tyler would have found something that made use of his English degree. At least, that was what his father supposed.

But no, Tyler found most doors closed to him for entry-level editing or writing jobs. The world was a competitive place for English majors, especially those who'd spent four years taking classes mainly in poetry, creative writing, and French literature.

So when Quality Investigations on north LaSalle Avenue offered him an entry-level job as an insurance investigator, Tyler jumped at the chance, even though he knew it would make little use of his degree (save for writing up underwriting reports on folks applying for large life insurance policies—but the wording of these was so proscribed that Tyler's English degree and writing aspirations hardly mattered). His father would at least be happy he'd found something with a degree that had been both an object of ridicule and disappointment for Dad ever since Tyler declared it in his freshman year.

Tyler swung his legs over the edge of his bed. He told himself he could work on his novel and short stories in the evenings. And he could always keep his eyes open for another job, something more suited to his creative and literary abilities.

He had to admit—he was a little excited about the prospect of his first day at work at a real job, no matter how boring and routine it might prove to be. Who knew whom he might end up working alongside? And the prospect of being a morning and afternoon commuter on the Metra train excited him—he could visualize himself in one of the green leatherette seats, wearing his crisp white shirt, rep stripe bowtie, and navy slacks, reading James Joyce as the suburban and urban landscapes blurred by his window.

Save for clerical work at his father's intellectual property law firm, Tyler had never worked full time before and the mystery of what awaited him in the real world was making him a little giddy with anticipation.

Who knew what might be out there waiting for him? Perhaps a new friend?

Maybe even a lover?

Tyler pushed away the sheet covering his hairless white frame and leapt from his bed.

Today would be a good day, a turning point.

*

Tyler paced outside the LaSalle Avenue high-rise that housed Quality Investigations on the building's thirty-second floor. He took off his glasses and gave them one more polish with the bottom of his shirt and then tucked the shirt back into his pants. He watched other workers, just like himself, hurrying both north and south on the crowded sidewalk.

The day had started off hot and humid and had only gotten more so as Tyler rode the train into downtown. Now, the air felt like a moistened blanket hanging over him, weighing him down. Despite the discomfort, he was suddenly nervous about heading inside to the little windowless cubicle he'd surely be assigned. His stomach churned at the prospect—exciting earlier—of all the new people he'd meet today and churned even more as he thought of having to make all the phone calls his new position would entail.

What had he been thinking? He could never do this job! He was the kind of guy who worked in isolation. The idea of having to talk to people all day made him break out in a cold sweat, in spite of the fact that the temperature was already in the upper eighties.

Buck up, old man, he told himself, adopting a plummy internal British accent. *Get yourself in there. Rise to the occasion. Chin up. Forward!*

*

"Tyler, I'd like to introduce you to Emory Hughes. He's been with us for more than five years. He does the same work you'll be doing, so I've assigned him to be your mentor for your first couple of weeks. He's here to answer any questions you might have about the work and to show you around the office, get you comfortable. Okay?" His supervisor, Jennifer Vidovic, beamed at him as though she were delivering a million-dollar bonus check rather than some coworker who most likely wanted to be anywhere but here.

Tyler looked up from his desk, where he'd been reading Quality Investigation's New Employee Handbook, to regard a mouse.

No, really, the guy reminded him of a mouse. There was something rodent-like in his looks—dun-colored hair, in need of a good cut, and the way his two front teeth were slightly longer than the others—Tyler expected the guy's nose to twitch. Yet, there was something bright in his pale-blue eyes that drew Tyler in. He was tall, too, which Tyler liked. His mother would say that he was "skinny as a beanpole," but Tyler liked that too. He favored tall, skinny guys and had found them to be reliably well-hung.

He banished these thoughts, and the laughter behind them, to an empty room of his mind, the one with the sign on it reading "later." He stood and, like the well-mannered young man he was, extended his hand for Emory Hughes to shake.

Without meeting his eyes, Emory gave Tyler one of the weakest handshakes he'd ever experienced, outside of his mother's Tuesday afternoon luncheon and bridge club when it was held at their house. "Hi, I'm Tyler Kay."

"Nice to meet you," Emory responded in a voice just above a whisper. Tyler had to lean in to hear him.

Jennifer swept her long bleached-blonde hair over one padded shoulder and eyed them. "I'll let you two get acquainted. Emory, why don't you take Tyler around and introduce him to everybody. I'll see you both in my office around noon." She grinned. "I'm taking you both out for lunch."

Emory watched her walk away. He turned back to Tyler. "She's too thin, drinks and smokes too much, and she is *not* your friend. Watch everything you say to her because she can and will use it against you someday. She keeps a journal called *A Day in Transition*, in which she catalogs all of our shortcomings."

Tyler took a step back. "Okay, then. And what are her good points?"

Emory rolled his eyes. "Don't be silly. Those *are* her good points. I'll save the bad ones for later, maybe after lunch. She'll take us up the street to Mr. Beef. I hope you're not a vegetarian."

Tyler shook his head. "Carnivore."

Emory smiled. "I like that." He moved into the hallway outside Tyler's cubicle. "Let's get these introductions over with, so I can go back to work. Jennifer will expect me to meet my quota, regardless of my mentoring duties."

"You don't have to do this," Tyler said, hoping he was being helpful. He had a suspicion Emory was as much of an introvert as he. "I mean, I'm sure I'll meet everybody on my own in the next couple of days anyway."

"No, you don't get it. I *do* have to do this, unless I want Jennifer to write me up for insubordination, which she will." He gestured with his hand for Tyler to precede him.

"We'll start in Underwriting."

Tyler followed, taking note of Emory's stoop-shouldered walk. There was something nerdy and sexy about the man. There was also something that reminded Tyler of Ichabod Crane.

*

After a pained lunch brightened only by the amazing Italian beef sandwiches they wolfed down, Tyler was granted a brief reprieve from his new boss, when Jennifer announced she was taking a cab back. "There's room for all of us," she said, when she saw the yellow cab heading north on LaSalle. She moved toward the street, skinny arm aloft.

Emory spoke up. "Okay if Tyler and I walk back?"

"In this heat?" Jennifer shook her head and pursed her bloodred lips. "It's a sauna."

"I don't mind the heat so much." Emory glanced over at Tyler, who stood next to him. "You don't mind, do you, Tyler?"

"Not at all."

Jennifer glanced down at her watch. "Well, if you get back any later than 1:15, you'll need to make up that time. I'd prefer you do it today before you clock out."

Emory smiled. "I wouldn't have it any other way. And neither would Tyler." He elbowed him. "Right, Tyler?"

"Right." Truth be told, Tyler would have been happy to have taken the cab. The heat and humidity were oppressive. His clothes would wilt. His hair would curl. He just might melt into the pavement. But, at the moment, Emory was the one he wanted to impress, or at least be agreeable toward, so he didn't want to argue.

After the cab took Jennifer away, Tyler began the walk south with Emory at his side. Now that they were alone, Tyler couldn't think of anything to say, which wasn't unusual. Jennifer had chattered on and on at lunch, about a new diet she was on, the TV shows she'd set her VCR to record, her cat Miss Marples, and how she and her "damn feline hunger" never let her sleep past 4:00 a.m.

Tyler actually preferred self-centered, loquacious people like Jennifer Vidovic. They took the pressure off him to say anything. He could relax. Because, unless he had a script, Tyler's mind often went blank when called upon to speak.

They'd walked for several blocks before Emory finally spoke. "You follow the news?"

Tyler shook his head. "Not much. I like to read."

"Newspaper, then?"

"Mostly novels. Right now, I'm rereading Oscar Wilde's *The Picture—*"

Emory cut him off. "How do you get your news, then?"

Tyler shrugged. "I don't, I guess. I figure it'll get to me if I need to know about it."

Emory said nothing for another block or so. They were almost to their building.

As they headed toward the pair of revolving doors, Tyler figured he had nothing to lose, so he grabbed hold of Emory's arm. Emory stopped suddenly, just short of the revolving doors and looked down at the hand on his arm and then up at Tyler. His mouth opened and closed, as though he were about to say something; then he went silent.

Emory pulled his arm away.

The reaction made Tyler think twice about proposing what he was about to put out there. But, damn it, he was pretty sure this guy was gay, and Tyler was lonely. All his friends from high school were either clueless as to Tyler's "true" identity, or they were away from home, chasing after advanced degrees or the good life in New York, Miami, Los Angeles, anywhere but Chicago.

Emory, weird as he seemed, might just be a good match.

So, mouth dry, and feeling a little shaky inside, he asked Emory, "Hey." Tyler swallowed, determined to see this through. "You, uh, wouldn't be interested in maybe grabbing a drink with me after work tonight?"

Emory looked at him as if he'd just proposed jumping off one of the downtown bridges spanning the Chicago River.

"Or another night if tonight isn't good." Tyler glanced down at the toe of his Florsheim loafers and then back up at Emory. He felt like his smile came out more on the sheepish side than the welcoming one.

Emory shrugged. "I've got a sick mom at home. Let me check in with my sister and make sure she's home to see to her. If the coast is clear, why not?"

Tyler felt a sense of relief. It wasn't a no, after all.

*

At the end of the day, Tyler had just hung up the phone from an interview with a man who'd moved down to Florida after winning his state lottery. He felt more than heard someone standing behind him.

He swiveled in his chair to find Emory, shifting his weight from one foot to the other.

"Hey!" Tyler called. He stood to look out at the bright July sky. "Did you talk to your sister?"

"What?"

"You said you needed to be sure she'd be around to take care of your mom? Just wondered if you could join me for that drink."

Emory nodded. "Yes. I think that would be nice. You ready?"

Tyler nodded. Most of the office had already headed out, but he could see Jennifer still in her office on the perimeter of their work space. She had a door and a window and everything. Her back was toward the door as she hunched over her desk.

Emory picked up on the glance. "Yeah, we better get out of here before she sees us. I guarantee she'll run up to one or both of us." Emory then spoke in a high-pitched, surprisingly good imitation of Jennifer's voice. "Oh, could one of you boys be an angel and do this one tiny thing before you head out for the night?" He then shifted back to his normal, velvety-soft voice. "And then we'll be stuck here until seven or eight o'clock. Trust me."

Tyler laughed and grabbed his sport coat off his chair back. "Let's go. I know just the place. And we can walk."

*

They were on State Street, just north of the river. Tyler was a little young for Sing Hallelujah, whose patrons were mostly middle-aged and older men, but the bar was the closest one to their office. Closest gay bar, anyway. Sing Hallelujah was also near the Grand Avenue subway stop. Tyler knew, from their conversation at lunch, Emory took the L home. Tyler was considering doing the same. The L subway was a lot cheaper than the Metra commuter train—and would certainly have more interesting characters to contemplate on the long journey home. Fodder for his stories...

"Well, here we are," Tyler halted in front of the bar's unpretentious entrance, a simple green-painted door in a weathered redbrick façade. Sing Hallelujah shone in neon script from one of its black-tinted windows. "A piano bar. I know it's a little corny. Showtunes and singalongs and all that. But they make a great G & T."

Emory eyed him and Tyler read suspicion in his gaze.

Tyler smiled. "Is everything okay? We can go somewhere else—"

Emory cut him off. "This is a gay bar."

Tyler felt heat rise to his cheeks. Had he misread the guy? He was usually good at picking up the signals. You had to be, these days. He let out a little laugh. "Is that a problem?"

"I'm not gay." Emory's expression was one Tyler had trouble reading, other than understanding his new coworker was *not* happy with him.

Tyler tried to lighten the mood. "Oh, that's okay. They'll let you in anyway. No judgment here!" He chuckled.

"I don't want to go to a gay bar." Emory started to move away.

"Wait! We can go somewhere else. I just wanted to have a drink, get to know each other a bit outside the office, you know? This was close and, and...my sister comes here." Tyler didn't know why he'd added that last part. Susan had never set foot in this bar, far as he knew. Susan had never set foot in a gay bar, period. Not that she had anything against them, of course. She'd always been on the side of her "homo little brother," but then she liked the same things Tyler did—hairy chests, big dicks, broad shoulders, and jaws sculpted from granite. Because she was unlikely to lay hands on any of the above at an establishment that catered to "the gays," she'd never patronize one, unless Tyler dragged her in.

And he'd yet to try that. He didn't need his sister cockblocking.

"Is your sister gay?"

Tyler scratched his head. "Uh, no."

"Then why would she come here?"

Tyler felt a little sick to his stomach. Emory seemed suddenly confrontational and pissed off. "I dunno. She likes how strong they pour their cocktails and appreciates a good Sondheim tune?"

Emory cast his gaze down at the sidewalk. Tyler had hoped he'd at least laugh, but his little joke seemed to sail right over his head. When he looked back up, he asked, "Are *you* gay?"

That caught Tyler up short. What if the guy was some homophobe? He was his mentor at work, for Christ's sake. Tyler castigated himself internally for his rush to judgment about on which side Emory's bread was buttered. And what should he say now? How could he make things right? "Um, we could head on up to Rush, if you want."

"Where all the singles clubs are?" Emory grinned, but there was something unkind in it that chilled Tyler despite the heat surrounding them.

"Yeah."

Emory cocked his head. "You still didn't answer my question."

A long pause followed. And, although he moved in a world that wasn't exactly welcoming or even friendly to his kind, Tyler had never hidden himself from anyone, not even his own conservative family. It was a matter of principle. So he forced himself to meet Emory's gaze and said, "Yeah, I am. Gay as a picnic basket. I could be the love child of Paul Lynde and Charles Nelson Reilly."

Emory didn't laugh, as Tyler had hoped he would. "Wait. Do you have a problem with people like me?"

If he did, that would be that, Tyler thought. He'd make the best of their time together at work, knowing

Emory's mentoring gig wouldn't last forever. And, hey, he at last felt—if Emory had a problem with who he was, then that was *his* problem. Tyler had no reason to hide from anyone, including this guy. He wasn't ashamed.

After a long pause, Emory shook his head. "No. I get it. You can't help yourself, right?"

Tyler wondered if he should be offended. But the truth was—no, he couldn't help himself. "Well, no more than I can help having blond hair or being five foot ten. I am who I am, Emory." He exhaled a long breath. "Look. I read things wrong. I apologize."

He was about to go on when Emory raised his hand. "Wait a minute. You thought *I* was gay?"

Tyler sensed a yes to that question wouldn't be the wisest answer. "I don't know, Emory. I didn't really think about it. I just picked a place I knew of that was close to work. It's not a cruisy place. It's a singalong piano bar, friendly to everyone. Now, we can go in and have a drink, get to know each other a little better. Or we can head off in separate directions. It really doesn't matter to me. I didn't mean to shake you up. And bringing you here wasn't, in case you're worried, some master plan to seduce you."

Emory's mouth opened a little.

To reassure, Tyler hastened to add, "I have no master plan. I just thought we could be friends."

Emory nodded. He looked up at the sign in the window. Just when Tyler thought he was about to turn and walk away, he said, "Okay. What the hell?"

Tyler didn't move.

"Are we going in?" Emory prompted.

"Sure." And Tyler opened the door for him.

*

Tyler hurried back to the high-top table where they'd planted themselves. It was next to a high-up, rectangular window. As he set their drinks on the scarred surface of the little round table, Tyler noticed Emory checking things out through the dusty window. He wondered if Emory worried about being seen. "They're all tinted, so we can look out, but no one can look in. No worries. Okay?"

There was a Tanqueray and tonic for him and a coke for Emory.

"I don't drink," Emory had told him as he headed off to the bar. Tyler wondered for only a second why Emory had agreed to come out to a bar. Why not suggest they go out for coffee, instead? But what Emory drank or didn't drink really wasn't Tyler's concern, beyond his wish that the guy would loosen up a bit.

"Thank you very much." Emory traced a finger along the side of the glass, damp with condensation. He leaned in to sip through the straw.

Tyler took a big swallow of his own drink, taking note of the fact that the bartender poured his drinks strong. He was an affable, fiftyish guy named Vern with thick black-framed glasses, sporting an orange and cream caftan. Tyler had to hold his breath to keep from choking. Old Vern must have only whispered the word tonic into the glass. Tyler would need to go very easy on the cocktails if this first one was any indication. He felt awkward enough as it was.

Now that they were here and settled, Tyler found he had little to say. After all, he'd only known Emory for eight hours or so, and almost all of their exchanges had been about the work they both did.

Yet, after their confinement in the stultifying office environment, the last thing Tyler wanted to do was talk more about work—even if it was juicy gossip—so he turned to Emory and asked, "So...what you do you like to do for fun?"

Emory sipped his coke. "Fun. What's that?"

Tyler laughed but stopped when he realized Emory wasn't even smiling.

Emory shrugged. "I'm sorry, Tyler. I shouldn't be such a stick in the mud. It's just that lately my life has revolved around my mother. She's very sick and, even though my sister doesn't work, I somehow have ended up being her caretaker. I don't want her alone in some AIDS ward—" Emory stopped himself short.

Even in the dim light of the bar, Tyler watched his cheeks redden, read the desire to take back what he'd just said. He rushed in to be supportive, compassionate. "Your mom has AIDS?" Tyler cocked his head. He reached out to cover one of Emory's hands with his own, but Emory flinched and pulled away.

Emory nodded. His face had paled, and he looked...well, how could Tyler describe it? Deflated? Numb? "She does." He took another sip of his drink. "You wanna know how she got it?"

Tyler felt a little sick to his stomach. "You don't need to share that." He wondered if there was a story about a drug addict mother or one who slept around. "I'm so sorry to hear this. Is she getting treatment, being helped?" He'd heard about AZT and how it was working for some people, but knew little about it. Tyler would admit, even if only to himself, that he had his head buried firmly in the sand when it came to the twentieth-century plague. He was always careful, of course, even to the extent of sometimes asking his partners to "double bag" before they fucked him, but he'd yet to get tested himself. He didn't see the point.

And, to be honest, he was more than a little afraid of what the result might be.

Emory shook his head. "We tried AZT, actually. For four days. Four days of diarrhea, vomiting, and horrible nausea. It was making her sicker than she already was." He smiled sadly. "And that was really, really sick." He drained his coke and asked again, "You want to know how she got it?"

Hoping maybe an interruption would change the course of this conversation, Tyler stood and grabbed both glasses from the table. As he moved to the bar, he noticed the vintage disco and video playing. A bunch of dancers gyrated in tight red shorts on the big screen mounted above the bar. *That's what I wanted to come out for. Just a little fun. Some lightheartedness.* He set the glasses down, and Vern came over after making change for a guy with a frosted pompadour across the bar who was trying, Tyler thought, to make eyes at him. He looked up again at the video—Sylvester on the screen, belting out how someone made him feel "mighty real."

"Two more, please." He was about to ask Vern to tone down the amount of gin but decided against it. The way things were going, he might need the liquor a lot more than the restraint.

When he settled back in on his stool, shoving Emory's coke across the table, he could see that Emory waited for him.

"She had a car accident. Mother." He leaned in again to sip from his straw. When he looked up again, tears shone in his eyes, but there was no hitch in his voice when he spoke, no trouble with his breath. "It was a few years ago, on Lake Shore Drive. Up at the curve? Where it turns into Sheridan?"

"I know it," Tyler said, because he felt like an answer was expected of him.

"Head-on collision. You know the story, drunk driver going too fast, weaving in and out of lanes just to get to his destination a couple minutes earlier than he would have if he hadn't been speeding. Mother was coming home from her bridge club that night. They met at Ann Sather's, on Belmont?"

Tyler nodded.

"It wasn't horrible. I mean, she was hurt, cut up really bad...and bleeding. That's why she needed the transfusion. She'd lost so much blood at the scene. She had a transfusion, and they did some stitches. We brought her home the next day, thinking everything would be fine."

Tyler took a big gulp. He imagined what was coming.

"It took three and a half years. Three and a half years before we noticed anything was wrong. That first little purple spot, on her arm, was the signal. It seems so innocent now. Mary Helen and I just thought it was a bruise or maybe one of those blood blister things you get." Emory smiled and Tyler noticed a weird light in his eyes. Was it pain? Anger? Fear? He didn't know what to say. Didn't know, in fact, if it was necessary to respond at all.

Emory's story seemed like a dam opening up, unleashing. He wondered if Emory had ever shared it before.

"We ignored it, but then they started to crop up in other places—on her calf, one on her neck. The biggest one was right near her armpit and Mother's always been a bit vain, so she hid that one. She started waking up at night and complaining that her sheets were soaked. We didn't know anything, really, until the pneumonia. And the fever. When it went up to 104, we took her to the ER. By then, she was struggling with diarrhea and had lost twenty pounds." Emory smiled, but there was no joy in the expression. "Mother's what some people politely call, 'a big-boned gal,' so we didn't notice the weight loss. Not right away. Neither my sister nor I dreamed Mother had AIDS, for heaven's sake. That was a disease for—" Emory stopped himself and met Tyler's gaze. "Sorry." Emory drained his drink and watched out the window as a city bus went by and then a jogger with a Walkman, its orange foam headphones against his ears. "I know you probably don't want to hear this, but let me just get it out."

"It's okay, Emory. Tell me whatever you need to. It's a shame about your mom." He bit his tongue to keep from adding something like, "It just goes to show you that the virus doesn't discriminate."

Emory drew in a quivering breath. "They came and told us—my sister and me—that Mother might have the virus. They'd tested and they'd come back negative, but there was this thing. A window period? Where you could show up negative. They told us to get her tested again in six months, just to be on the safe side, you know? They were concerned because her symptoms were what they called classic. Mary Helen and I looked at each other, confused, because back then we didn't even know what words like seroconversion or window period meant." He grabbed hold of Tyler's hand for a moment, which surprised him, but he clung to it, clutching it tight, as he finished. "That was the beginning of the nightmare. Since then, she's just been on a downhill slope, moving slowly but surely toward the end, I know."

"Isn't there something that can be done?"

"You really don't read the newspapers, do you?"

"What?"

"If you picked up a paper once in a while, or even turned your TV on, you'd know there's nothing to do for this horrible plague. Sure, there's AZ-fucking-T. That might help some people, but it did *nothing* for Mother.

"Now, she's dying in her room. Wasted away to nothing. Hallucinating sometimes. I think that fever in there is just eating her brain up, bit by bit. It's like a demon." He shook his head and regarded Tyler with what Tyler perceived as unvarnished disbelief. "And you say you're gay? Yet you're so ignorant about this disease that's taking so many... Every single day."

Fevered heat rose to Tyler's cheeks. He looked up at the TV above the bar, which was now playing the video to some Donna Summer song, continuing the disco showcase. He couldn't even make out the lyrics because the blood rushed so hard in his ears. "I'm sorry," he mumbled.

Emory didn't say anything for a while. Then he stared at Tyler, hard, for a few moments, his lips compressed into a thin line. "Okay," he said, voice barely above a whisper. "You're sorry." He shoved his glass away from him and as he did so, it tipped over, spilling ice cubes across the table and onto the floor.

It seemed Emory hardly noticed. He stood quickly. Tyler gasped as coke and melted ice cubes cascaded onto his lap.

Emory said, "I'm sorry too." He looked around the bar, as though he were looking for a familiar face, someone to rescue him. "I have to go. Mother will wonder what's keeping me."

Before Tyler had a chance to respond, Emory turned and strode quickly from the bar, leaving Tyler wet, confused, and thinking, too late, of what he might have said or done.

Chapter Four

Emory wandered the downtown streets for a while before heading to the Grand Avenue subway stop. Because it was only a little after six, there were still lots of commuters hurrying to and fro along the sidewalks, all of them looking depleted and wrung out by the summertime heat and humidity. He didn't see one smiling or remotely friendly face. Everyone looked miserable, beat. Emory wondered why anyone chose to live in this city by the lake—with its unbearably damp and hot summers and its unbearably brutal winters.

He thought of Milwaukee, just to the north and how it was also on Lake Michigan, but appeared to be smaller, friendlier, less stressful than Chicago. Maybe he should move up there, once he got free.

His thought on that topic brought a grim smile to his face. *I could rent Dahmer's apartment. Now that it's available...*

The last thought made him feel horrible—guilty.

That freedom he suddenly realized he so craved would mean his mother had finally passed on to the great beyond, where she would find her skin magically restored and liberated from the crusty lesions that plagued it. If she was aware enough to realize what she looked like—and why her own daughter cruelly referred to her sometimes as "Spot"—she would have been mortified. Mother had always been a proud woman. "I never apologize for being overdressed," she'd once told him. This was a woman who put on foundation, mascara, and lipstick to walk to the corner store.

Even though Emory did pray for his mother to die, to be released from her suffering, he didn't know if he could bear the hole in the world that would surely be left behind by her absence. It was a conundrum he could bring no resolution to.

Just before he got to the Grand Avenue subway and the smelly stairs that would take him down to its subterranean world, he came across one of those squat boxes from which one could purchase a newspaper. The blue box was dedicated to the *Chicago Sun-Times* and the picture on the front page made him stop, suck in a breath. He looked around a little before stooping down to look at the paper behind the Plexiglass window.

There he was, once again, Jeffrey Dahmer. He'd been lifted from obscurity, from the darkness of his private deeds, to national headlines. He looked so—what? Deer caught in the headlights? Nonplussed? Afraid? No, not afraid, just maybe, well, *resigned.*

He had to have known this fate was coming. He couldn't have expected to go forever without being caught.

He gleaned a few more details—how Dahmer had a fifty-seven-gallon drum for bones from the bodies he cut up, how he'd sprayed skulls he kept on an altar gray to make them look like plastic replicas, even how he'd admitted to frying up and eating the bicep of one of his victim's—before standing up and wiping his hand on his pants.

He groped in his pockets for change, but had none.

He walked away, thinking he'd read enough anyway. No one was watching him standing there, absorbed by the article. He glanced around to make sure of it.

Down the damp concrete stairs and into the subway he went. A phalanx of commuters, a mix of races, ages, and sexes filled the platform. It must have been a long time since the last train had rolled into the station. Emory leaned against a tile wall, trying not to breathe in the musty air, but grateful for the mildewed chill being underground provided.

Or was he feeling a chill because of what he'd just read? He shook his head. *Leave it to the media to play up the most horrific details, to call Dahmer the Milwaukee Monster, to revel in the salaciousness of it all.*

He pushed the thoughts out of his head and forced himself to move from the security of the tiled wall to the edge of the platform, where he could peer into the blackness of the empty tunnel to look for any sign of an imminent train. He looked down as movement caught his eye—a rat scurrying along the tracks.

He hoped it wouldn't be electrocuted by the third rail. He watched as it progressed into the tunnel, the shadows swallowing him up.

He felt more than heard the rumble of the oncoming train. Because of the number of people already waiting, he knew he'd be crammed inside a car, body-to-body, with a bunch of sweaty strangers. There'd be no seat for him. He'd be lucky if he even was able to squeeze into the open doors.

The prospect made him feel a little sick to his stomach.

Why had he even agreed to go for a drink with the new guy?

He needed to get home to Mother and Mary Helen.

*

He paused in the vestibule of his building to claim that day's mail. Mary Helen, of course, couldn't be counted upon to even do this simple task.

Junk and more junk, but at the bottom of the stack of circulars, bills, and a come-on to join Triple A, there was a hand-addressed envelope. He turned it over, heart hammering, but could find no return address.

He hurried up the stairs with the mail in one hand, his keys in the other.

It took him more than one try to get the door open. And when he did, he flung himself down on the couch and, with shaking hands, tore the letter open. He went immediately to the signature at the bottom of the page.

It was signed "Jeff."

Emory closed his eyes. *Oh my God, he wrote back. He wrote back.* He didn't trust himself to see what Dahmer had written, fearing that maybe his response would be a curt brush-off, or perhaps a heavily redacted missive, so full of blacked-out words and phrases as to be unintelligible.

Look. Just look.

And he did. The note was short, but there was nothing there to fear.

*

Dear Emory,

Thanks for reaching out.

You took the time to write to me and give me a

civil word. Believe me, that's a rare thing for someone in my shoes.

I'm so glad you understand. We monsters need love too!

I hope you'll keep writing. I could use a friend, especially when the whole world is against me. I don't even know how long I'll last in jail even though I keep company with thieves, rapists, and murderers. Somehow, I find myself below even them in the prison ranking system. I'm the lowest of the low, even in the worst of company.

Everyone wants to see me dead.

Everyone except you, I hope.

Keep in touch.
Jeff

*

Emory stared down at the letter, then reread it. Reread it a second time, then a third. He couldn't believe how easy it was to forge this connection with one of America's most infamous people. He felt, for a moment, removed from his bland and wretched existence, singled out and special.

He would write again tonight.

Now, though, Mother needed tending to—cleaning up and deciding what to feed her, even though she'd most likely eat very little or none of it. Maybe he'd just open a can of tomato soup. She used to love that, paired with a grilled cheese and a dill pickle spear. The last two components were out, way out, these days, but perhaps Mother could choke down a spoon or two of the soup.

He was headed toward the kitchen when he paused in his tracks. He thought, beneath the lingering smell of Mary Helen's Marlboro smoke, he could detect a different and strange odor—something sweet, vaguely nauseating.

Had Mary Helen gone and left the refrigerator door open again? She'd done it so many times in the past that he'd given up on reminding her about it. She didn't pay for the milk and the meat that spoiled when she didn't check to make sure it was closed before heading out for a mysterious day or night, so why should she care?

When he got to the small kitchen, the refrigerator door was firmly closed. And when he opened it, it looked as though it had been shut the entire day. The shelves were cold, as were the few things inside—the half gallon of milk, the package of Oscar Meyer bologna, the starting-to-mold carton of strawberries. Emory grabbed the berries and sniffed them. Although there were several spots of mold, they didn't smell bad. He dumped them in the wastebasket underneath the sink.

No, this smelled more like rotting hamburger.

Emory shrugged. It was hot. The apartment didn't have air-conditioning and neither did most of their neighbors. What he was smelling was most likely garbage outside wafting in through the open windows. Another joy of summertime in the city.

He pulled out the battered saucepan from the cupboard under the counter and then emptied the contents of the soup into it. He set a medium flame beneath it, then crossed the kitchen to grab the milk so he could gradually stir in a canful.

When everything was ready, Emory took out a tray from a different cabinet under the counter and placed a bowl of the soup along with a glass of ice water, a spoon, and some saltines on the tray.

He carried it to his mother's room.

The door was closed and he rolled his eyes. Another thing he'd asked Mary Helen to do over and over was to leave Mother's door open when she left the apartment. Mother could then at least look out into the hallway, or maybe the wind would contort itself enough to at least give her a cross breeze.

Mary Helen always rolled her eyes when he mentioned this to her. "She doesn't know if that door's open or closed, doofus. She doesn't even know where the fuck she is."

It hurt Emory's heart to hear his sister talk about their mother so dismissively, so cruelly.

Pausing outside his mother's door, he sniffed again. The odor seemed stronger here, and it was definitely rotting meat, sickeningly cloying. He suddenly thought of what he'd heard on the TV news about Dahmer and how neighbors had complained about the odd odors emanating from his apartment.

The notion made Emory shiver.

He carefully balanced the tray as he opened the door.

Mother sat up in bed and smiled as he stood framed in the doorway. "Oh, my sweet boy! What did you make for Mother today?"

Emory was stunned at the change. She'd slipped into a clean nightgown, a lavender nylon one decorated with a pattern of irises, her favorite. A purple barrette Emory had never seen held back her gray hair, which this evening seemed more lustrous, maybe even fuller, if that were even possible.

She had color in her cheeks and her eyes, usually a jaundiced yellow with broken veins, had suddenly morphed and were now clear and bright, sparkling.

The nightstand beside her was clear of medications and now there was only the little milk-glass lamp she loved and the gargoyle she'd made back when creative juices flowed through her veins, rather than a deadly virus.

Emory wanted to drop to his knees and thank the Lord for this miracle.

"Why, I made you tomato soup, Mother. I know how much you like it." He crossed the room and set down the tray on the foot of her bed.

"I hope you fixed it the way I prefer it."

"With milk instead of water? You bet."

"I'm hungry!" she squealed. She held up her arms so he could set the tray on her lap.

But when he glanced down at the tray, he realized he'd forgotten something. "I need to run out to the sideboard and get you a napkin, dear. I won't be a minute." Mother couldn't abide paper towels or even paper napkins, calling them uncivilized. There was a stack of worn linen ones in a sideboard in their dining room. He hurried to fetch one to spread out over her clean bodice.

When he returned, things were no longer the same. And Emory let out an involuntary hiccup of grief when it hit him that what he'd just seen was a hallucination, a product of desperate wishful thinking.

He knew at once from where the odor he'd noticed earlier was coming.

Mother lay in her bed, rheumy eyes cast upward at the cracked plaster ceiling, with its cobwebs and water stains. Her hands lay at her sides. Although she didn't have the zest of his very realistic daydream, Emory could at least console himself with the fact that Mother at last looked kind of—peaceful.

As he neared her bed, he wondered if he was experiencing even more hallucinatory sensations because it seemed all the sound in the world had stilled, in reverence or perhaps deference to this moment. Gone were the sounds of the wind in the Catalpa trees outside the window, the cacophony of the traffic zooming south on Kenmore, the calls of people to one another, greeting or yelling at each other in the torpid heat.

It was dead quiet, Emory thought, and then laughed morosely at his pun.

When he reached Mother, he stopped, his hand poised and hovering just above her face. He closed his eyes for a moment. *Please God, don't let her be dead. I know I've wished for it dozens of times, but only as an end to her suffering. Let the breath come back into her. Even as my greatest burden, she's also my greatest love. I don't know how I'll abide the hole in the world she'll leave behind.*

His prayer was useless, but he sent it mentally heavenward anyway.

He drew in a deep, yet quivering, breath before opening his eyes.

Mother continued to lie still before him. Her glazed-over pupils didn't move to the side to take him in. Her chest didn't miraculously begin to rise and fall. She didn't reach out, as she sometimes did, calling him "my boy" in a weak croak.

He bent a little as he pressed a hand to her forehead. He snatched it away with a sudden jerk, almost as though he'd been burned. But it was just the opposite—Mother's forehead was ice cold, despite the heat. Whatever once had thrummed inside her, warming, had gone away, slipping out her screened bedroom window while Emory was at work, ironically writing up underwriting reports for those who needed life insurance.

As though life itself was a quantity that could be insured, like a diamond ring, or a house, or a Porsche.

He stood for a moment, simply staring at his dead mother, remembering the times when she'd drawn him into her lap to read him yet another chapter from the series of old *Wizard of Oz* books they had in the hallway bookcase, or when she would insist on ironing his shirts and pants to ensure he was presentable to the world, or when she'd sit at the kitchen table, peeling and slicing Granny Smith apples for one of her famous apple pies that tasted better than anyone else's because she added a hint of maple syrup and brown sugar to the apples, along with handfuls of walnuts and raisins. He recalled crawling into bed with her when the thunder and lightning got too loud outside or when he'd awaken, screaming, from the nightmare of a strange man in his bedroom, a shadowy figure standing silently over him.

He remembered being *loved*.

And now that sensation, that security, was gone.

The lump in his throat grew so large it was hard to swallow. Tears burned in his eyes as though they were not simply salty water, but acid.

He leaned over, forcing himself to kiss Mother's cold, cold cheek.

And then he rushed from the bedroom, pausing only enough to draw the door closed—softly—behind him.

He threw himself down on the couch, expecting torrents of tears, hiccupping sobs, breathless weeping, but found he felt nothing but a curious numbness.

He wondered if this was what shock felt like, this emptiness.

He sat unmoving on the couch as the sounds of the world gradually filtered back in, the traffic and the music of voices on the street, as the shadows lengthened, steadily laying claim to the room, until he was by himself, in the dark.

Alone.

He didn't know when he'd fallen asleep, but all at once he woke to a sudden brightness, jarring, as the overhead light came on, flooding the room with a harsh yellow glare.

"What the fuck are you sitting here in the dark for?"

Emory sat up more. He'd slumped over when he'd fallen asleep. He rubbed his eyes and turned to look up at his sister.

Her lips were twisted into a smirk as she returned the gaze. All at once, he could see contempt, ridicule, and shame on her features.

She had no idea.

Yet.

"You should get to bed, Emory."

"What time is it?"

"It's a little after midnight."

Emory eyed his letter from Dahmer, still lying open on the coffee table. It became imperative to him, even more imperative than telling Mary Helen that Mother had passed away, that she not see the missive. He snatched it up, folding it so he could slip it into his pocket.

He licked his lips, tried to reach down inside himself for just a smidgen of composure.

"Sit down, Mary Helen."

She'd moved to the windows that looked out on the street. He could hear a car idling outside, and it occurred to him that someone might be waiting out there for her.

Maybe he should simply let her go without telling her. She didn't care, anyway.

She turned. "Why?"

"Because I have some news."

He heard the car drive away, taking with it a snatch of laughter, dying on the spare breeze.

She plopped down on a ladderback chair across the room. "Is it Mama? Is she okay? Did you have to call an ambulance?" For a moment, he saw the human side to his sister, the vulnerable part she hid successfully most of the time. It made his heart ache.

He patted the couch next to him. "Come on and sit beside me, dear."

She laughed, but there was fear in her eyes, the hurt, the need to avoid the news he was certain she knew was already hurtling toward her.

"Why?" She lit a cigarette and blew the smoke at the ceiling. She was attempting a look of nonchalance, and failing.

"Put that out. Just come sit beside me." He reached out to her with the plaintiveness of his gaze and, miracle of miracles, she did exactly as he asked. For once.

Next to him, he recoiled at the smell of cigarettes and alcohol wafting off her. Drink oozed from her pores. He wondered, for just a moment, if his sister was an alcoholic.

"She's gone, sweetheart. I came home and found her."

He sat with her in silence for several minutes.

And then she fell into his arms and, together, they wept.

It struck Emory that this was the first time in who knew how long he'd simply hugged his sister, felt her close. It made him even sadder to contemplate that it was their mother's death that brought this nearness about.

After a time, Mary Helen sniffed, sat up straighter, pulling away from him at the same time. She wiped her nose on the palm of her hand and then rubbed at her eyes. They were red and glistening.

"What are we going to do? What will we do now, Emory, without our mother?" Mary Helen asked, and in her troubled voice, Emory heard the little girl she'd once been. The one who had looked up to him like the father they'd never known...

"Well, we'll need to call an ambulance. We'll need to figure out the arrangements for her."

"What if they won't take her?"

"What do you mean?"

"You've heard the horror stories, Emory. About people with...with her disease."

Emory shook his head. Without knowing if he was right, he said, "That won't be a problem. Folks are beyond all that, now."

But are they?

"Oh, I'm not so sure."

Emory eyed the phone on the end table. "Should we call an ambulance now?"

Mary Helen didn't say anything. He'd never seen her look so lost and confused.

"Can it wait? Just until the morning?"

Emory had been thinking the same thing. He wondered how long Mother had been lying dead in her room. It could have been since early the evening before, when he'd last checked in on her before heading off to his own bed. That length of time, he thought, would account for the smell.

And the smell would only get worse. But it was late, so late, and what difference would a few more hours make?

"I think we can wait."

Mary Helen sat up straighter. "I want to go in and see her."

He closed his eyes, imagining her grief, and nodded.

Emory simply sat still, his head reclining on the back of the couch, as his sister left the room. He expected a gasp or maybe even a scream, but all he heard was the creak and soft close of the door to Mother's room. He waited a while. The door closed and opened again. The rush of water from the bathroom, the squeak of the cabinet where they kept the towels opening and closing...

He'd thought Mary Helen wouldn't want to stay with Mother for long. A word of goodbye, maybe, a too-late proclamation of love, and then off to her own room. Who knew if she'd even stay the night? She was gone so much lately he wondered if he could truthfully even say that she'd lived here.

But what he sensed was at least a half hour gone by with no sound from the back of the apartment. He pushed himself up and off the couch to see what was keeping Mary Helen.

He crept down the hallway and swung Mother's bedroom door open slowly, quietly.

The room was dark. Wan, pale light from the crescent moon outside filtered in. Mary Helen stood by the side of Mother's bed. On the nightstand, there was a bowl of soapy water. Mary Helen dipped a washcloth in it, wrung it out, and then applied it to their mother. She made long, deliberate strokes, cleaning her arms, her legs, at last her face, patting Mother's cheeks with tenderness. Mary Helen's brow furrowed in concentration as she worked. There was such love in this simple act.

When she finished, she set the washcloth in the bowl of soapy water and then looked over. She'd known all along he was standing there. Then, she cast her gaze away, sighed, and got into bed. She lay curled up like a baby next to their mother's body. She'd draped one of Mother's arms across her shoulders.

The scene should have repulsed him, released some primal prohibition against consorting with the dead, but all he felt was touched.

He didn't say a word, but simply backed from the room, closing the door behind him.

Let her have her time, he told himself as he made his way to his own room. *It would have been nice if she could have—even once—laid down and held Mother when she was alive, but at least it shows she has a heart, something I was beginning to doubt.*

Emory shut his bedroom door. He undressed quickly and then donned his pajamas. He took Dahmer's note from his pocket and placed it on top of his desk.

The world had shifted, but Emory moved to the bathroom. He still needed to perform his nightly ritual of brushing and flossing and washing his face. The world continued to turn.

Back in his own room, he sat at his desk. He picked up the letter from Dahmer and read it once more, imagining in this late-night hour, when all of Chicago was relatively quiet, that he could feel the killer's energy within the paper.

He let his mind drift away from horror and loss.

And then he began to write…

Chapter Five

"Emory won't be in today, so if you have any questions, just stop on by. My office door is always open." Jennifer smiled, even though she was telling a bald-faced lie; her office door was actually shut most of the time.

But he pulled back the thought because he'd seen something new in her face that he hadn't seen before—kindness. It put him on alert and made him suspicious.

"Oh, is he okay?" There'd been talk around the office that morning that a vicious summertime flu was making the rounds.

Jennifer leaned against the work surface of Tyler's cubicle and stared straight ahead as she said, "His mother passed away."

"Oh, no. That's so sad. He was just telling me about her."

Jennifer eyed him. "He was? Did he say what was the matter? I couldn't get any details out of his sister when she called to report him off."

Tyler knew enough not to share what he knew with her. "I don't know. He just said she'd been sick, and he'd been taking care of her." Tyler shook his head. "Poor guy." He looked at his computer screen, the blue background with the white letters on it. The rectangular cursor blinked at where he'd left off in his report, as though tapping its foot impatiently. "Are we doing anything? Maybe sending flowers?"

Jennifer stood up. "Oh, honey, that's a sweet thought. But there's no money in the budget. But you can certainly do so, if you're inclined." She thought for a moment and Tyler wondered if she realized how heartless she sounded. It was amazing how quickly she could shift from kindness to indifference. "I'll stop by Walgreens at lunch and pick up a card that we can all sign."

"That'd be swell," Tyler said, wanting to draw the words back in as quickly as he'd blurted them out, dripping with sarcasm as they were.

Jennifer didn't seem to notice. Without another word, she left him alone in his cubicle.

Tyler felt more troubled about the loss than he thought he had a right to, given the limited time of his acquaintance with Emory. *But when do our feelings ever follow a logical path?*

He promised himself he'd call a florist on his break at ten thirty. He was sure Jennifer would pass along Emory's address. And with that latter thought, Tyler had an idea.

*

Tyler had never been in this part of Chicago before. He was a suburban boy and knew only the more popular areas of the city, frequented by suburbanites and tourists—Wrigleyville, Grant Park, the Loop.

Now, he stood on Granville Avenue just after work. The L that had just dropped him off rumbled out of the station above his head. He looked around and saw a lively neighborhood. There were coffee shops, a couple bars (he'd heard of the Forge, a gay bar, but was always told to avoid it because it was "an old man's bar"), a laundromat, some other small businesses. Toward the east, the buildings soared up to the sky—high-rises on Sheridan

Road. To the west was the hustle and bustle of Broadway—more traffic, more restaurants and bars.

He pulled the Post-it Jennifer had written Emory's address on from his pocket. He lived in the block of Kenmore just north of Granville. A few steps to the east and around the corner, really.

Tyler passed the Sovereign Hotel and mused that it looked more like an apartment building than a hotel.

And then he was at Emory's. He didn't know why, but he expected Emory would live in a smaller building, perhaps even a two-flat or a three-flat that you see everywhere in the city.

Emory's building was an older high-rise, fashioned from weathered red brick. Tyler stood just outside the awning over the glass front doors and guessed the building must be at least twenty stories tall, maybe more. The views of the lake and the city from the top floors must be awesome, but Emory lived on the first floor, so what he saw would most likely be the street, parked cars, and the backs and sides of other apartment buildings.

Tyler went into the lobby and located Emory's name on the directory. He took a deep breath and buzzed.

Emory's voice, a bit garbled came through. "Yes? Who's there?"

"It's Tyler, Emory." Tyler shouted.

"Who?"

"Tyler Kay, your coworker."

The silence after that stretched on for so long that Tyler worried that Emory was ignoring him.

But, at last, a jarring buzzer sounded, startling Tyler. He hurried to grab the door as he heard the lock unclick.

He dashed through the lobby to the elevator at its rear. He pressed one, even though they were on the ground floor already, but the first floor was above that.

The elevator opened onto a long, red-carpeted hallway with brass sconces on the wall at regular intervals. Tyler thought it might have looked nice at one time, but now, the subtly-striped wallpaper looked dated, in some places water stained. The light fixtures could use a cleaning and some needed replacement bulbs. The carpet was worn lighter in the middle where residents trod.

The whole place smelled of cooking grease, cabbage, cigarette smoke, and God knew what else.

It was hot.

He was yanked out of his reverie as a door opened down the hallway. Emory's head poked out. His hair was disheveled, and he was dressed in an old gray sweatshirt with the sleeves cut off and a pair of faded jeans. Despite being the very essence of neatness at work, Emory actually looked better this way, younger, sexier. More normal.

Tyler pushed the thoughts aside and smiled. He held up the bouquet of daisies he'd bought for far too much at a little florist's shop on Michigan Avenue.

"What are you doing here?" Emory asked.

Tyler started toward him, letting the flowers clutched in his hand precede him. "I heard about your mom. I just wanted to stop by real quick to offer my condolences."

Emory eyed the flowers, then looked up at Tyler, almost as though he were confused about this small gesture, unused to kindness. He stepped out into the hallway and then pulled the door almost closed behind him. He reached out to take the bouquet. Holding them at his side, he thanked Tyler. "It was thoughtful of you to do this. You didn't have to."

"I know I didn't. I wanted to."

Silence crept in between them and seemed to be considering staying a long while. Tyler felt awkward and wondered if he should simply offer another few words of sympathy and then be on his way.

And yet, there was something so lost and lonely in Emory's features that Tyler felt compelled to do more. He knew it was bad manners, but he asked anyway. "Can I come in?"

"Now's not a good time," Emory said.

Tyler shrugged. "That's cool. I just thought you might like a bit of company."

Emory said nothing in return. He simply crossed his arms and stared at Tyler, waiting.

Tyler shrugged. "Well, I guess I should be on my way. Home. To Wilmette." He smiled.

Emory nodded.

Tyler had wondered, on the train, if he should offer Emory a hug. Now, he realized a physical gesture wouldn't be welcome. So, he turned and started back toward the elevator.

Just when he was about to the doors, Emory called, "Wait! Where are my manners? Of course you can come in."

Tyler looked down the long hallway, feeling almost as though he were in a dream. Emory had opened the door widely and stood waiting, his hand on the doorknob.

Tyler hurried back and followed Emory into chaos.

First off, the apartment smelled really bad. A combination of smoke, rotting food, and some sickening sweet perfume that had probably been sprayed to mask the other odors hung over the place like a pall.

Compared to the large home Tyler came from in Wilmette, the apartment Emory shared with his family seemed ludicrously small, almost unlivable. He could see into the kitchen, where dirty dishes spilled from the sink onto the counter beside it.

The room they were in, the living room, was crowded with old, grandma-style furniture, all maple and chintz, that seemed too large. It made Tyler feel crowded, almost claustrophobic. A layer of dust on all the surfaces didn't help matters much either.

Tyler sneezed.

Emory picked up a newspaper from the coffee table, which was already crowded with used cups and plates, and tucked it under his arm. He smiled sheepishly. "Sorry about the mess."

"No, no. Don't be sorry. You're going through a lot. Would you like me to help you tidy up while I'm here?"

"No!" Emory's response was swift, almost panicked. He let loose a little titter and gestured toward the couch. "Have a seat. I could, uh, make some coffee or tea."

The temperature in the apartment had to be in the nineties. A hot beverage sounded revolting. "That's okay."

"Maybe something cold?" Emory turned and went into the kitchen. Tyler followed. He took note of the copper molds placed decoratively on the soffit above the sink, the white-painted table and chairs, the calendar from the year before on the wall. The cabinets were white metal, vintage fifties stuff.

Emory was bent at the waist and peering into the refrigerator. "Only we don't have much. No pop or iced tea." He kicked the refrigerator door shut. "Glass of water?"

"I'm fine, Emory, really. I just wanted you to know I was thinking about you. I guess I wanted to see for myself if you were okay."

Emory looked down at the flowers still in one hand and the newspaper still tucked under one arm. It had been a feat to even open the fridge and glance inside. He set the newspaper on the kitchen table, upon which a Tater Tot casserole sat, half-eaten, with a fly buzzing around it. He put the flowers Tyler had brought on the kitchen counter, thinking he'd find a vase for them right away.

"Well, it was good of you to come. Especially when it's so far out of your way."

"It's not. Just a quick on and off from the L. That's all." Tyler shifted his weight from one foot to the other. He thought he should go. He thought he should stay. Emory seemed to be here all by himself.

Tyler leaned up against the wall. "Um, have you been able to make all the arrangements?"

Emory nodded. "Mary Helen helped out with the details a surprising lot. She's my sister."

"Is she here now?" Tyler was having trouble imagining what Emory's sister might look like. A female version of Emory?

"No. She's moving out." Emory paled as he spoke the words. "She, uh, she's moving in with, um, a friend."

Tyler cocked his head. "Okay. So you have the place all to yourself now?"

Emory looked panicked. He swallowed hard. "I guess. Not sure I'll be able to afford the apartment without Mother's social security. May need to find a little studio. Maybe Rogers Park?"

Tyler tried to put a positive spin on things. "Well, that could be a fresh start." He smiled. "I could help you move, if it comes to that."

Emory waved him away. "I don't know what's gonna happen, really. I have to look at my budget. This place, obviously, is pretty cheap, anyway. The landlord hasn't updated since we moved in twelve years ago."

"That long? You must have been children."

Emory moved to the window and turned his back to Tyler as he stared out. "It *was* a long time ago."

The nostalgia in his voice suddenly made Tyler want to weep. Here was a man, he thought, who suddenly found himself all alone in the world. And, even if his mother was sick and dying and his sister an enigma, at least he had *some* family.

"Where did your sister go? Mary Helen?"

"She's gonna be living over in Andersonville?" Emory said, mentioning the old Swedish neighborhood clustered around Clark and Foster. He looked at Tyler for a long while, as though debating whether to share. "She's a lesbo. I had no idea until she told me she was moving in with her girlfriend, now that Mother had passed. She said there was nothing to tie her to this place anymore." Emory looked down at the floor, then back up at Tyler. The admission seemed to revolt him. "Sorry. I don't mean to sound bitter or judgmental. I know you're gay too. It's just that it came as something of a shock. She was never around these days, but I figured she was just a whore." A short bark of laughter, bitter, escaped him, like even saying the word whore was scandalous.

Tyler said, "Well, even lesbians can be whores." *Why did you say that? At a time like this? What's wrong with you?*

But Emory laughed—way too hard for what the situation warranted. He laughed until the tears came, until he was holding his belly, breathless. When he had control of himself again, he said, "I suppose you're right."

They fell silent then. And Tyler began to think there was no more to say. He reminded himself once again that he barely knew this guy. And yet, he felt for him. Emory's loneliness radiated off him like a wave.

"Have they had the services yet?"

"What services? You mean like viewing hours and all that? A minister at the gravesite, reading from Psalms? Making her lie down in green pastures or something like that?"

Tyler had no response. Had he asked the wrong thing?

"We didn't do any of that. For one, Mother didn't want it. So, Mary Helen and I scraped enough together for a pine box and a quick cremation." Emory's face took on a curious blank aspect that made Tyler want to take him in his arms, to let him know that it was okay to cry, to lean into his grief, but he stayed rooted to the wall he leaned against, almost as though physically restrained.

"We'll get a box with her 'cremains,' that's what the funeral guy called them, 'cremains.'" Emory chuckled. "They'll give us a call. We can pick Mother up then." He waved toward the living room. "I can bring her home, put her on the mantel. She'll keep me company." He laughed, but the mirth didn't reach his eyes. "At least now, she'll be quiet. For a change..."

Tyler was a little breathless, oppressed by the heat. Or maybe it was the whole bizarre situation causing him to feel as though he couldn't suck in enough air? He suddenly felt a need to get out, *now*, but it was tempered by the nurturing side of him, the side that had come here wanting to help a friend in a time of need.

"You had your dinner yet? Can I take you out for some food? I saw a diner on the way over here."

"That's nice of you. Maybe another time. You should be getting home."

"Okay," Tyler said uncertainly.

"Okay."

It was as though Emory was waiting. And maybe he was.

Tyler hurried through the apartment and paused at the front door. Emory arrived on silent feet, just after. Tyler asked, "When do you think you'll come back to work?"

"Tomorrow," Emory replied, as though the answer were obvious. "We only get two days off for bereavement. I've used 'em. I need the money." He opened the door for Tyler. "I'll see you there, then."

Tyler smiled and debated once more whether he should give Emory a hug. In the end, he hurried out the door, and even though the hallway was worn down and dated, it felt like sweet freedom to simply be out of the crowded little apartment.

He was about to turn back to Emory to tell him if there was anything he needed, Tyler would be happy to help.

But Emory had already closed the door.

The Bartender

He waited around the bar all night for me to close up.

He'd had his eye on me from the first time I served him. He started out a shy boy, all innocent glances from beneath slightly lowered lashes.

But, as he drank more and more—and I'm not one to discourage this, especially when they're tipping well—he loosened up. The flirting became more outrageous, winking and even, one time, licking his lips as he stared pointedly at my crotch.

I threw him a couple free drinks only because he seemed lonely. The fact that he was fixated on me helped too.

And then, when closing time rolled around and I shouted out my standard cliché, "You don't have to go home, but you can't stay here," he didn't move. The lights came on. The music on the juke box, Crystal Waters "Gypsy Woman" ended.

I wiped off the bar a final time and reached below it to get my backpack.

"We're closing, friend. Didn't you hear me announce last call?"

"That song? The one that was just playing? So dumb to sing about the homeless like that. It trivializes them."

I nodded. "You got a point there."

I hoisted the backpack over one arm and then moved out from behind the bar. I looked at him and smiled. "Got to lock up, set the alarm. The owner doesn't allow customers in here while I do that."

His face reddened. "Sorry." He hopped down from his stool. "I got all caught up in just watching you."

I paused. "You're sweet." I touched his cheek and gave him a little peck on the lips. He stepped back, stunned, but he was thrilled. You know, sometimes my tips aren't in crumpled ones and change.

I motioned with my head toward the door. "Dude. You gotta go."

He nodded. "Okay." He stood by the door for a time, watching me.

The slightest tinge of annoyance prompted me to point toward the door. "Now," I said, smiling to soften the blow.

"Yeah, sure." He opened the door and outside— freedom.

The night's mine now. Granville Avenue is flooded with an orangeish light from the streetlamps. An L train passes overhead, and I swear I feel the vibrations through the soles of my combat boots. There's a couple of guys arguing outside. One's shouting about the other's "wandering eye" and says he'll never be able to trust him again. I shake my head. How many times will I overhear variations on this same fight?

The more things change, the more they stay the same.

The train makes me wonder what I should do next. I could head south, grab a nightcap, a boy for the night...

The door slams shut. I'm alone. I go back behind the bar and grab a glass, pour myself two fingers of Jack Daniels, and down it.

Fortified, I open the door and emerge into the night.

I'm heading toward where I'd left my car parked on Winthrop when a voice calls from the alley running behind the bar. "Hey. Where you headed?"

I stop and backtrack a few steps.

It takes a moment for my eyes to adjust. The alley's filled with shadows. But I recognize him, barely separate from the dark, leaning against a dumpster. He's got his pants undone and his hand's inside, working. I consider moving on, but what the hell? I can fool around with this guy, get my nut, head home, and get a good night's sleep for once. I'll save myself a few bucks on drinks too. Save even more if I'd end up going to the baths, which is what I'd probably do if I strike out at a bar.

I pause, looking to my left and my right. No one's around. It won't be the first time I've hooked up in an alley, and the street's quiet for now. I think of this one time when I got a blowjob from a cop while a rat watched from beside the dumpster.

I move into the darkness, smiling, my hand whispering across the faded denim of my crotch, already anticipating the buttons being undone.

He gets on his knees as I draw closer.

Chapter Six

Emory locked the door and threw himself down on the couch. It creaked under his weight. He surveyed the room through Tyler's eyes, and it came up badly wanting. It was a hellhole, a pigsty, not fit for human habitation.

When had it gotten so filthy?

He'd have liked to have blamed Mother and her illness, but that wasn't true. Not anymore. Once she got sick, everything went to hell in a handbasket—that much was true, but she could hardly be blamed. Once upon a time, Mother would have both he and Mary Helen cleaning on Saturday mornings—dusting, vacuuming, polishing, washing windows—until the place shone. Back then, there was a real pride of ownership, even if they were only renters.

But once she was no longer able to supervise and was confined to her bedroom, Emory and Mary Helen let things slide. And there was no excuse! The dust accumulated. Bed linens seldom got washed. The floor felt gritty if you walked barefoot across the creaking hardwood. The cockroaches seemed to be multiplying—and becoming bolder.

It had been kind of Tyler to take the time to stop by, to actually bring him flowers. Other than the old lady who lived down the hall, Mrs. Schermerhorn, who'd come over with a casserole yesterday, no one else had visited. Mary Helen and her girlfriend, a flannel-shirt-wearing stereotype with a crew cut, named Liz, had stopped after the cremation to gather up Mary Helen's things, and as they put it, to "get the hell out of Dodge." They were packed up and gone within an hour.

Even though their relationship had been strained, veering on nonexistent, for the past few years, she was still his sister. He still loved her. He didn't know if he'd ever see her again.

And if he did, he wasn't sure he had it in him to forgive her for abandoning him, right when he needed her most. You'd think the death of the mother you had in common would draw siblings closer and not divide them further. But Mary Helen had been contrary for years. Sometimes, he believed she hated him.

He remembered when they were children. He was eight years older than Mary Helen and always looked out for her, almost like a surrogate father. He'd make up stories and games for her and dress her up in one of Mother's slips for dance parties in the living room when Lawrence Welk was on. They'd hunker down together in front of the TV and share a box of powdered sugar doughnuts while watching sitcoms on TV.

They were close. No one could deny it. And, even though Mary Helen was far younger than he was, she eased his loneliness. He was a tortured, bullied kid at school, the butt of every joke, beaten up regularly.

He had no friends.

He still didn't.

But when he had Mary Helen, when they were a pair, the pain of being an outcast would subside just a little bit.

Maybe that was about to change. There was Tyler, who seemed to take an interest in him, to genuinely care about his welfare. His sympathy and support felt weird. Emory didn't know if he deserved the attention or not.

There was Dahmer, in his prison cell. His famous buddy.

Thoughts of Dahmer reminded him he had yet to check the mail that day. He tapped his pocket, making sure he had his keys, and headed downstairs to the lobby.

The doorman, or what passed for one in this building, looked up from the *Newsweek* he was reading as Emory passed him.

"Hey Emory. Sorry to hear about your mom. You need anything?"

"Thanks, Pete. I'm good." Emory eyed the dark-bearded man, wanting to look into his dark-brown eyes, but didn't dare.

"She was a good woman, your mother. A real lady. You don't find many of those anymore."

Emory nodded. He wished Pete would shut up. Emory was afraid if Pete continued, he'd start crying, and he wasn't about to do that in front of the doorman.

Barely looking at Pete, he gave him a small smile. "Nice of you to say so. Mother would have appreciated the kind words."

Pete nodded and went back to his magazine.

In the mailbox, Emory found the Commonwealth Edison bill, the phone bill, a two-for-one pizza deal from Giordano's, and a letter from a prison in Wisconsin. This last made Emory smile, genuinely, for the first time in days.

Pete grinned as he passed through on his way to the stairs at the back of the lobby. "Good news?"

Emory stopped smiling abruptly and hurriedly slid the prison-sent missive under the Giordano's flyer. "Free pizza. I think I'll order one tonight. Mother never allowed us to have pizza." He laughed. Pete cocked his head and didn't join in.

Emory raced up the stairs and back to his apartment.

He dropped everything but the letter on the coffee table. He took it into his bedroom.

After tearing open the envelope, he lay down across the bed and began reading.

Dear Emory,

Thanks for writing back so quick.

Your letters keep me sane. Alive.

Sorry about your mom. Were you close to her? The less said about my mom, the better.

I know it's hard, but you need to get out, so you can get over your grief. Chicago has a lot of distractions (I remember). Maybe find some...

Jeff

Emory had hoped for more. He felt as though he could see into Dahmer's very soul and expected the same depth of feeling back. He'd written Dahmer a four-page letter when he'd found Mother's body, telling him how alone he was in the world now, and how she didn't deserve this virus she'd ended up with. He'd confessed his confusion and his fear for his future.

He let Dahmer's reply slip from his fingers to the sheet beneath him.

Outside, the sky was painted in the colors of twilight—pale gray, lilac, navy blue—and yet encroaching night brought no relief from the humidity and the heat. Emory wriggled out of his clothes, flinging them on the floor, and then got up, naked, to move the box fan from the window. He placed it on one of the dining table chairs he had in his bedroom and positioned it at the foot of his bed.

If he was going to be even a little productive at the office tomorrow, he needed sleep. His eyes burned and his body ached for it, yet he wasn't sure he'd succeed. Still, he lay on the damp sheets, trying to ignore the grit from his dirty feet at the bottom of the bed.

He lay, trying not to think, for what seemed like hours. Sweat dribbled down his smooth chest. Even with the fan blowing hot air on him, it still felt suffocating, as though the walls were closing in, the ceiling dropping. And, as he might have predicted, the harder he tried to go to sleep, the more awake he felt, despite the weariness in his bones.

At one point, groggy, he could have sworn he saw Mother standing in the shadows in the corner of the room.

He tossed. He turned. And at last, he sat up, thought about what Dahmer had said—about getting out.

There's no one around anymore to care about where I go... When I leave and when I come back.

Emory rummaged through his closet and brought out a pair of jeans and a plain white T-shirt. He slid into them and found the off-brand sneakers he'd bought earlier that summer from the Payless over on Broadway when he'd had the idea he'd begin running along the lakefront.

It was as though he'd had his destination in mind before he even realized it. There was a siren call, maybe or maybe not inspired by Dahmer, and he could hear it loud and clear because it was only down the street and around the corner.

He set off.

Emory knew if he hesitated for more than a minute or two outside the Forge, the gay bar on Granville, he'd never go inside. He'd passed the place many times, even glimpsed into its dark and smoky interior when his passing by and the door opening coincided. The smell of beer and smoke would waft out, borne up on men's voices and disco on the jukebox.

He waged a war with himself ever since they lived in the neighborhood about going inside, just to "check it out." But so far, the side he called his decent side, had won out and he'd never set foot in the door. But now, he told himself he'd already been in a gay bar in the recent past, so why not go in another?

Dahmer had told him to seek out the "distractions" in his city. And if ever there was a time for distractions, Emory thought, now was it. He needed distraction from loss, loneliness, and the feeling there was no one else like him in the whole world.

The place was dark, but not so dark he couldn't see every eye in the place turn Emory's way when he walked in. The bartender, a bald guy with a Fu Manchu mustache and wearing a leather vest and tight jeans, paused in drawing a beer from the tap to eye him. Except for one man, sitting in the red light from the jukebox near the end of the bar, all ten or so patrons swiveled their heads to take a gander at the fresh meat.

Emory froze in the doorway, afraid to move, afraid of breaching some unknown bar etiquette.

But he had to move. It would be too awkward to simply back out now and even more awkward to just stand there, with his "thumb up his ass" as Mary Helen might say.

So he took a few quick steps to the closest stool at the bar and perched on it. The bartender shot him a lopsided grin and hurried over. "What are you having tonight, handsome?"

Emory had to resist the urge to look behind himself for this "handsome" stranger. He smiled back and managed to find his voice. He'd seen ads for Miller beer, the champagne of beers, on TV, so he asked for one of those.

"We have it on tap or in bottles. Which can I get you?"

Emory wanted to ask if there was a difference in taste but resisted that impulse too.

The bartender added, with a wink, "Tap's cheaper. Tonight, we're having a quarter special."

"It's only a quarter?" Emory asked, failing to keep the surprise out of his voice.

The bartender nodded. "I can see we don't have a spendthrift here. I'll get you a nice, frosty mug."

He turned and Emory tried and failed to force his gaze away from the rise and fall of his ass in those tight, faded-to-nearly-white Levi 501s. He watched as the bartender pulled the beer, letting the golden liquid slide up the side of the glass, and when it was nearly full with a perfect white head on the top, he set it before Emory along with a napkin.

"There you go. You wanna run a tab?"

Emory immediately thought of the pink cans of Tab his mother used to drink and then giggled. He shook his head and groped around in his back pocket for his wallet. He pulled out a dollar and set it on the bar. "Thank you." He took a sip of the beer and decided he liked it.

The bartender took the dollar and asked if he wanted change. Emory did, but he shook his head. This gesture earned him another wink from the bartender, who stuck out his hand. "I'm Eric. Just whistle if you need anything else." He set a bowl of peanuts before Emory. "I haven't seen you in here before."

"That's because I've never been here." Emory took another long swallow. The beer was refreshing, especially after suffering the heat outside. They had the air-conditioning cranked up, which was a blessing. The chill was delightful, even if he did have to put up with the stench of cigarette smoke. About half, or maybe even more, of the patrons had cigarettes burning. A pall of blue-gray smoke hung just below the black, painted-tin ceiling.

"Well, I hope it won't be the last time we see you here, sexy man."

Emory felt heat rise to his cheeks, and his mouth dropped open.

"Don't look so surprised. You're hot. I hope you come back."

"Hey, Eric! My glass is empty!" A fat guy in a yellow tank top whined from across the bar, and Eric went to quiet him.

Emory was glad to be alone. The bartender, frankly, frightened him.

As he drank his beer and took in the other patrons—all what he'd call middle-aged men—it surprised Emory that they all looked what he would call normal. *Nobody in here seems swishy. Maybe this isn't a gay bar after all.* He quickly dismissed the latter thought when he focused on how the bartender had shamelessly flirted with him. Plus, there was the fact that the walls were decorated with black-and-white photographs of wildly muscled men, shirtless, in locales like garages, factories, and leaning against eighteen-wheelers. Sweat glistened on their bodies, even in the dim light. Emory hoped no one caught him staring, slack-jawed, at the figures. They caused a fluttering in his gut, weird, and an erection to rise in his jeans. He reached down—he hoped subtly—to adjust himself.

He paused with his beer midway to his mouth when he noticed what was on the news on the TV mounted above the bar. The sound was muted to accommodate the jukebox, someone wailing about how they'd survive, but the picture of Jeffrey Dahmer, in prison orange, caught his eye.

Several other men turned to stare up at the screen as the newscaster's mouth moved in front of the image of Dahmer.

Someone nudged Emory. He turned and noticed the guy sitting next to him for the first time. He was relatively young, probably only a few years older than Emory himself. He had blond hair and a wispy beard and mustache. His eyes were a pale blue, and he wore a ribbed tank top, cargo shorts, and Converse high-tops.

"They should lock that guy up and throw away the key, don't you think?" He took a sip of some clear cocktail. "Or better yet, cut him up like he did to his victims. What a sicko!"

Emory leaned back, recoiling. Shakily, he drank from his mug and then set it down, too hard, on the bar. "I thought, in this country, folks are innocent until proven guilty."

The guy snorted. "You shittin' me? Oh, I think the body parts in his fridge were proof enough. Or maybe that gallon drum of whatever acid he used to dissolve the flesh of his victims. That's pretty convincing, eh? Or maybe those skulls he kept?" He looked Emory up and down. "Man, are you nuts?"

"Maybe I am," Emory gathered himself up, feeling indignation. "Jeff's a friend of mine. You just don't understand him."

The guy eyed him for a long moment. "I don't need or want to understand him. He's a monster."

Before Emory could argue any more on Dahmer's behalf, the guy picked up his drink and moved half a dozen stools away. He continued to eye Emory and leaned over to whisper something to the man next to him, who looked at Emory and frowned.

Emory hunched over his beer. This was a bad idea. He'd come to the wrong place and didn't belong here—didn't belong in a gay bar, period. *So what have you been doing in them lately? Deny much?*

"Don't worry about them. They all hate themselves, Emory. And they'll take it out on you."

Emory looked over at what had been an empty stool, its seat covered in black vinyl and patched with duct tape.

Now the stool was occupied by a man who looked so familiar, it took Emory's breath away. He had short blond hair, stubble, and wore a gray hoodie in spite of the heat. On his face was a look of amused, but weary boredom.

"You can't be. You're *not*," Emory stammered. With a shaking hand, he lifted his mug and drained the beer in a long swallow that ended with some of it dribbling down his chin. Irritated, he wiped the suds off his face and raised his hand to order another.

Eric filled another mug, set it down in front of Emory, and took it away with no indication that a man who looked exactly like the most famous serial killer in the country was seated next to Emory. "Thirsty boy," Eric said.

Emory threw another buck on the bar and waited until Eric was busy helping other customers—a couple who'd just come in—before speaking again.

"Not who? Not what?" The man gave him a sly grin.

"Never mind." Emory gulped down some more beer. And, because he was not used to drinking, he began to feel the effects of the alcohol—a little pleasant dizziness, a fuzziness.

"You look an awful lot like—"

The guy cut him off. "Don't say it! Let's not attract attention."

"Okay." Emory glanced at the other patrons. It was getting more crowded as the hour grew later. Yet no one seemed to notice that Emory was seated next to a man who could be Jeffrey Dahmer's twin.

"Okay," Emory repeated, grasping for something else to say. "What brings you out tonight?"

He smiled. "The same thing that brought us all out, I guess. Looking for someone special. If not Mr. Right, then a Mr. Right Now." He laughed. "Am I right?"

Emory chuckled, but the alcohol, combined with a strong feeling that he'd slipped unwittingly into *The Twilight Zone*, made sitting here in this run-down, hole-in-the-wall bar seem unreal, like he was dreaming.

And maybe he was.

Perhaps he had drifted off to sleep and would awaken at first light, the sheets beneath him damp with sweat, and the image of Dahmer's face imprinted on his memory.

"I don't know what I'm looking for. Certainly not Mr. Right. Or Mr. Wrong. Or whatever. I don't even know if I'm gay." Emory snorted, wondered if the guy would think he sounded like a fool or some self-loathing imbecile who had so little awareness of himself that he could make such a claim with a straight face.

"Oh, you're gay all right." He winked. "Anybody can see that."

"Really?"

The guy nodded. "Doesn't make you a bad person."

"No, no, I guess it wouldn't," Emory responded. "I just haven't figured things out yet."

"You have. You just haven't come to terms with them yet."

Emory felt shaky—angry but scared and exposed too. "Oh, what do you know? We've never even met."

"Haven't we?" The man raised his eyebrows. Emory noticed he had no drink in front of him.

Flustered, Emory blurted out. "I need to use the restroom. Excuse me." He slid from the stool and hurried toward the back. He rushed inside, grateful that the red-painted bathroom was a single and he could lock the door behind him. He crouched on the edge of the toilet without taking down his jeans and covered his face with his hands.

You are losing it, man. Losing your fucking mind.

He drew in several deep, quivering breaths, letting them out with a sigh. *That's not him. It's not. That's not even possible. It's just someone who looks like him. And he's aware; he knows it. He's fucking with you.*

Someone tried the doorknob, rattling it, and Emory jumped. He got up and rinsed off his face.

When he opened the door, he discovered no one waiting outside. Nobody even loitered nearby.

I need to get home. It's got to be going on one or even two. I have to work early in the morning, for crying out loud.

He hurried back to the stool he'd occupied, expecting to say some words to the guy, to maybe offer an excuse for his hasty departure, but there was no one sitting on the stools on either side of him. He took a long look around the bar. Not one guy there looked like Dahmer.

Odd. There was a fresh mug of beer at his place, untouched.

He caught Eric's eye. "I didn't order this."

Eric shrugged. He didn't seem as friendly as before. There was a coldness to his stare. "You don't want it?"

Emory shrugged. "It's okay. I'll drink it." He climbed up on the stool and took a sip. He wanted to ask Eric who'd bought the beer for him. He needed to know if he'd seen where his lookalike acquaintance had gone.

But Eric had turned his back to him, washing glasses in the sink below the bar.

Hadn't anyone else noticed the bizarre resemblance? Wasn't anyone else as shaken as Emory? But the bar seemed blissfully unaware of the guy's existence. They were blissfully unaware of Emory too.

And maybe that was for the best.

He finished his beer, ordered another one.

And another....

*

Emory awoke with a start, tangled up in his top sheet, naked. Mother stood near him, back turned, dressed in a pink suit with a pillbox hat.

"Mother," he mumbled, rubbing the sleep from his eyes. "You look just like Jackie Kennedy."

She turned. The front of the dress was splattered with blood and brain matter.

Emory shrieked.

And he awoke, for real this time, to bright sunlight streaming in through his window. Dust motes danced in the air. A tiny little man, situated just behind his eyes, pounded on them with an ice pick, begging for release or at least relief.

Emory had slept naked, something he never did.

Emory burped and jumped from his bed, hand clasped over his mouth and made it to the bathroom just in time to throw up into the toilet. All that came out was yellowish bile that smelled of hops. He slumped back against the wall, stomach still heaving, face slick with sweat, and watched a cockroach skitter across the black-and-white tiled floor.

The vomiting had at least given him some relief from the nausea, even though the headache still pounded in beats, timed to his pulse, just in back of his eyes. He glanced up at the old Herman Miller wall clock and saw that if he didn't hurry, he was going to be late for work. So, he crawled from his place against the wall over to the clawfoot tub and switched the hot and cold water taps on. He waited until the water was a comfortable temperature and then flipped the switch for the shower. Gripping the side of the tub, he stepped in under the spray.

As he turned under the warm water, he tried to recall what had happened last night. One thing he knew for sure—he had no recollection of climbing into bed. Indeed, he couldn't remember how he got home from the bar.

As he washed, he noticed more mysteries—his hands were scraped raw, as though he might have fallen at some point. When he moved the shower curtain aside and looked at himself in the medicine cabinet above the sink, he gasped. His left eye was swollen, and a red-and-purple bruise was making itself at home just beneath. He fingered it gingerly, wincing at the pain a feathery touch produced.

As he dried off, an image came to him, and he didn't know if it was real or if he imagined it. But in his mind's eye, he saw a falling star in the inky eastern sky, rocketing downward toward Lake Michigan.

He dressed hurriedly and set out for the L.

As he walked down Granville, there was a commotion in the alley behind the Forge. The whole alley was alive with cops and their vehicles. Crime scene tape. The squawk of police radios. Whirling blue lights.

And worst of all, a body on the ground, covered, but still it was obvious this had been a person. The sight of it turned Emory's stomach once more, and he gripped the brick wall for support, heaving, and praying he wouldn't throw up again. But the body just lying there in the grease-stained brick alley, surrounded by discarded trash, made his heart lurch as well.

A young woman, in a teal-blue sundress and oversized sunglasses, also watched the scene, her jaw dropped in horror.

Emory leaned in to her to ask, "Do you know what happened?"

She jumped at the sound of his voice.

Am I invisible to everyone?

Her dark eyes appraised him. "A guy got killed here last night. Or I guess it would be early this morning, from what I'm hearing."

"Does anyone know who it was? Someone from the neighborhood?" Emory's mouth was dry. "How did it happen?"

She shrugged. "I imagine they'll cover it on the news." She looked him up and down, and Emory felt she found him wanting. "I got to get to work." Her voice was barely audible.

Emory took one last look at the shrouded body and then made his way to the train.

*

It wasn't until he was headed home that Emory got some answers. In the lobby of his office building, a vendor sold magazines and newspapers from a little kiosk. Emory picked up a *Sun Times* for the ride home.

The story made the lower half of the front page. Emory grew sicker and sicker as he realized he knew the guy who'd been killed in that alley. His name was Eric Nowak, and he lived on the city's west side, in Norwood Park.

He'd worked as a bartender at the Forge bar, on Granville Avenue, for the last three years.

"What are you having tonight, handsome?"

There was a picture of Eric Nowak, but without knowing details, Emory would have never recognized him as the one who'd served him the night before. The picture, maybe a high school graduation photo, showed a clean-cut young man with curly blond hair and pale-blue eyes. He wore a sport coat and tie. This Eric was nothing like the bartender who'd waited on him, with his Fu Manchu mustache and shaved head.

People can change a lot in a very short time.

This was the same guy. It had to be.

What happened to him?

And where did the time from last night go?

When Emory got to his front door, there was a letter propped up against it. One of the neighbors must have gotten it in their mailbox by mistake. Thank God, they didn't open it.

It was another missive from Dahmer.

Chapter Seven

"I don't know what to think about him. Or, maybe, what I should *do* about him." Mary Helen lit a cigarette and blew the smoke at the fan in the window, which only sent it back their way.

"Your brother?" Liz pulled the sheet up over their sweaty bodies and patted the bed. Their dog, Zorro, an odd mix of Labrador and Dachshund, all black, hopped up to join them.

"Who else?"

"I thought you were done with all that."

Mary Helen didn't blame Liz for the characterization. For months before her mother passed away, Mary Helen complained to Liz about how stultifying it was to live in the grimy little apartment with her older brother and the mom who was dying from AIDS. She'd railed about how she wasn't sure which of the pair was crazier. She'd wished aloud for her mother to die, couching it as kindness, an end to her suffering.

But the truth was, Mary Helen simply wanted to be free. It was a burden, living with all that pain and misery, especially when there was no way she could find to alleviate it. But leaving? She simply didn't have the heart to do it while Mother was still breathing.

She'd thought once death came, as it inevitably would, she could leave and never look back. But she'd forgotten one thing—deep in her heart, where she couldn't logically deny it—she really loved her big brother.

Emory had done his best to take care of Mother, seeing to her hygiene and getting some food and liquids down her when she could tolerate it. Mary Helen knew she should offer more help than she did, but the sight of their once-vibrant mother lying amid soiled sheets and not recognizing Mary Helen was simply too much. She didn't want to be cruel and uncaring, but it was all she *could* be, in light of the circumstances. It was an act of self-protection. She hated herself for the weakness, but what could she do?

And she hated that Emory was so lonely. She could see that he struggled with his feelings about being gay (Mary Helen could admit it, even if her brother couldn't).

In the end, after the cremation, Mary Helen had only wanted to escape, to flee her depressing surroundings. Liz had been bugging her to move in with her ever since they first started dating, back around the new year, but Mary Helen never felt that she should. Liz was much older, attentive, and kind, but Mary Helen never felt a spark with her.

And now, here she was, in bed with her, the TV on, a dog taking up too much space next to her, and Liz's portable TV running the eleven o'clock news on channel two.

Mary Helen slumped back against her pillow, edging closer to Liz, not to cuddle, but to give herself a little more space than Zorro allowed.

The news was on low. The voice of the anchor was a low rumble, making Mary Helen think of the teacher in the Charlie Brown specials on TV.

"Wait a minute." Liz said, aiming the remote at the TV and sitting up straighter in bed. Her eyebrows came together with concern. Mary Helen tuned in more.

There was a picture of a handsome young man behind the newscaster who was providing details about his murder. His body had been discovered early that morning in an alley behind the Forge bar, in the Edgewater neighborhood. Mary Helen's stomach turned as the newscaster described how he'd bled out in the alley, due to blunt force trauma to the skull.

"Oh my God," Mary Helen whispered. "That's right around the corner from where I lived."

Liz glanced over at her. She shut the TV off. "And I knew that guy."

"You did?"

Liz nodded. "We used to volunteer together at the Howard Brown clinic. He was a nice guy, maybe a little too promiscuous, but aren't all the men?" She shook her head. "What a horrible way to die. I wonder what happened?"

"You mean what he was doing in an alley in the wee small hours? I think we can guess." Mary Helen wished she could take back the words. They weren't fair. They were character assassination with no grounding in reality. "I'm sorry. He might have just been passing through the alley on his way home after his shift. Maybe he needed to piss. He might have been pulled off the street into that alley by the killer." Mary Helen shivered and recalled a time when she was walking home from work after dark, and a thug wearing a ski mask had yanked her into a parking garage beneath an apartment building. He flung her to the ground, and God only knew what was in store for her. She was saved by someone calling out from a building across the street. The thug took only her purse, leaving her a concussion and a lacerated tongue caused by her biting down when she struck her head.

"Ah, Eric got around, that's for sure. I wouldn't be surprised if he was hooking up with one of his tricks in that alley. Maybe that's who killed him. Someone who got his jollies, and then, afterwards, decided to go back to the self-loathing. Maybe they thought they could stamp out their own desires by killing a fag. Isn't that what this Dahmer was doing?"

Mary Helen felt the old pull she'd felt so long as she watched her mother die—the urge to flee.

"I don't want to talk about this anymore. But I'll say this: that Dahmer guy? I think his problem wasn't self-loathing. It was loneliness. I heard he killed those boys to keep them with him, in a way." Mary Helen shut out, very quickly, the gruesome thoughts of dismemberment and cannibalism that rose up.

"Oh, who knows why he did anything? He's sick. And nuts. Glad he's behind bars."

Mary Helen put out her cigarette and rolled over, away from Liz. She found herself putting her arms around Zorro and drawing him close.

And she thought of Emory. Lonely Emory. Lonely Emory, who couldn't accept who he was even though Mary Helen had clocked him as gay when they were children and he would play Barbies with her or create elaborate fashion drawings at her request.

Or the way he seemed to have no friends at all in the neighborhood, save for the little sister he adored.

He'd endured more than his fair share of bullying for his adoration of a little girl as they grew up.

And the worst part was that Mary Helen herself, as they grew, pulled away from her odd brother too.

That, she was sure, hurt him even more than schoolyard taunts and worse.

Her not standing by him had been the ultimate betrayal.

She wondered if he knew about the murdered bartender. Had he seen anything? Did the murder, so close to him, frighten him?

Maybe she'd call him. Maybe she'd stop by, check in on him. She should.

She fell asleep with good intentions.

She woke with them all forgotten.

Part Two

Winter

Chapter Eight

Tyler made his way over a bridge above the Chicago River. He was headed to work on this early February morning. The city's towers rose all around him, holding up a sagging whitish sky, pregnant with even more snow. It would begin falling, Tyler predicted, before he got to his lunch break, adding to the grayish, slushy mess already in the streets. He could smell it in the bitter wind. His face burned, frozen; the snot in his nose crackled when he drew in a breath. His eyes stung.

Like everyone else on that bridge that morning, he was unidentifiable, hunched against the wind and buried under scarf, gloves and a down-filled coat. Even with all of that—plus corduroys and a Land's End Ragg wool sweater underneath—he was freezing his ass off. His teeth chattered, steam poured out of his mouth and nostrils with every exhalation, and he wondered why he continued to live in this arctic city.

He paused in front of a little diner just a few doors up from the high-rise building that housed Quality Investigations. He could hardly believe he was coming up on six months of employment. It seemed like only yesterday he was just starting. Is this where he'd be trapped? Tapping out underwriting reports for the rest of his days in a kind of cubicle-locked purgatory? Was this how most people ended up? In dead-end jobs, never mind careers, where complacency made a person suddenly wake up and see that they'd squandered a lifetime?

He peered inside the steamed-up glass of the diner. A Formica-topped counter ran along the front of the restaurant with red leatherette stools. It had the standard black-and-white-checked tile floors. Booths opposite the counter. Behind it, a short-order cook presided over his domain, flipping eggs, bacon, and hash browns on a flattop grill. Tyler wondered why he'd never ventured inside.

He glanced down at his watch. He was early today by a half hour or so—enough time to go in and warm up with a coffee and maybe a cinnamon roll or breakfast sandwich.

He yanked open the door and breathed a sigh of blessed relief at the welcome rush of warmth immediately surrounding him. He thawed and water dripped from his outer garments.

A red-haired waitress in a harvest-gold nylon uniform shot him a world-weary smile. She reminded him of the waitress on the cover of the *Supertramp* album he'd had in high school—a living, breathing cliché with Aqua Net, blue eye shadow, and orthopedic shoes.

"Sit anywhere you like, hon. I'll be with you in two shakes of a lamb's tail."

Tyler had to laugh. Was she really like this? Or being ironic? Playing the waitress part?

He didn't know, and it didn't matter. He climbed up on a stool and pulled out one of the vinyl-covered menus in between a sugar dispenser and a paper-napkin holder. He knew what he wanted, but it seemed like the right thing to do.

In a couple of minutes, or two shakes, she was before him, pencil poised above her pad. "Hi, hon, I'm Emma, and I'll be taking care of you. Get you some coffee to warm up?" She glanced out the window. "I heard it was twenty below with the wind chill." She shivered.

"Coffee would be great."

She started away and Tyler called after her, "And can you do a couple of poached eggs on toast?"

She grinned, as though reading his mind. "Want the yolks broken?"

He nodded.

She called over her shoulder to the short-order cook, a man Tyler thought was imported directly from central casting because he looked so much like Vic Tayback from *Alice Doesn't Live Here Anymore*. "Adam and Eve on a raft—wreck 'em!"

No one laughed, and Tyler assumed he'd fallen into *The Twilight Zone* territory.

Emma reached down below the counter and pulled up that day's copy of the *Chicago Tribune*. "Eggs'll be up real quick, sweetie. You wanna read the paper while you wait?"

Tyler was going to say no because he really didn't have time for a leisurely breakfast, but he took the paper anyway, mainly because he thought Emma, for some unidentifiable reason, would be offended if he said no.

The day's top story on the front page caught his eye. The serial killer and cannibal, Jeffrey Dahmer's, trial was wrapping up. Only yesterday, forensic psychiatrist Park Dietz, had testified and said that Dahmer wasn't suffering from any mental illness. *Right. The things he did? And he's not suffering from mental illness?* Tyler shivered. The forensic psychiatrist backed that up with the claim that Dahmer "had gone to great lengths to be alone with his victim and to have no witnesses." There was more than enough evidence that Dahmer prepared for each murder, therefore. "His crimes were not impulsive."

And that makes him sane?

Dietz had gone on to testify that, although Dahmer was often intoxicated when he was with his victims, "If he had a compulsion to kill, he would not have to drink alcohol. He had to drink alcohol to overcome his inhibition, to do the crime which he would rather not do." Dietz also said Dahmer identified with evil and corrupt characters from *Return of the Jedi* and *The Exorcist III*, pointing out the power held by some of the characters in these movies. Dahmer would actually watch the two films before seeking out a victim. Dietz diagnosed Dahmer with "substance use disorder, paraphilia, and schizotypal personality disorder."

Tyler shoved the paper aside. *Put whatever label you want on him. I'm kind of partial to nutcase and monster.*

His eggs arrived, their yolks spilling out onto buttered white toast.

Tyler's appetite suddenly vanished. He caught Emma's eye and again felt an irrational fear about offending her, so he asked, "I didn't realize I have a meeting to get to. Can you make my order to go? If it isn't too much trouble?" He smiled what he hoped was a winning smile.

She began gathering up the plate, the cup of coffee. "Sure thing, hon." She set the stuff on the counter behind her, tallied up his check, and then put that in front of him.

Tyler took cash out of his wallet, making sure to leave a big tip for Emma.

She was back "in a jiff" with a Styrofoam box and his coffee poured into a matching cup with a plastic lid. "There you go. Don't work too hard today." She winked.

"I'll try my best." Tyler hopped down from the stool and then gathered up his takeout.

"See you tomorrow!" Emma called.

"Right."

She held up the paper. "You want to take this with you?"

Just looking at the paper with its headline about Dahmer made him shiver once more. "That's okay."

He hurried out. There was a homeless man dressed in an old Army jacket and fingerless gloves shivering just outside his office building entrance. Smiling, Tyler handed him the food and the coffee. The man looked down at the containers and then back up at Tyler. "Bless you, man."

Tyler hurried through the revolving doors. As he waited for the elevator, he wondered what Emory would have to say about the latest news on Dahmer. Emory was like Tyler's dad with the Cubs, endlessly fascinated and, yes, oddly, endlessly in thrall, almost as though he were rooting for the killer cannibal's eventual triumph. Emory claimed he corresponded with the killer, but Tyler knew he had to be lying.

He'd gotten to know Emory a lot better over the past few months and the association hadn't always been easy. In fact, as Tyler rode up in the elevator to their floor, he marveled once again how close he'd come to the shy young man.

They'd had a very rocky start, with Emory pushing Tyler away every time Tyler would come close, whether that nearness was literal or figurative. What allowed them to find some sort of common ground was Dahmer and Tyler's love of horror movies and novels.

Tyler would have guessed his outpouring of sympathy over the loss of Emory's mother would have been the trigger to draw them closer, but although Emory seemed to appreciate the flowers and visits, the expressions and inquiries of concern and compassion, it was nightmare territory that actually brought them together.

Tyler paused just outside the elevator doors to recall that moment in the lunchroom, only the week before, when they seemed to strike a sort of accord.

I crept up behind him and glanced over his shoulder. For once, he was reading a newspaper that wasn't local. This was an obviously used edition of The New York Times *someone had left behind on one of the tables. The headline read, "Jury Hears How Unruffled Dahmer Dodged Arrest."*

The subject had come up between us before, quite a lot. Emory seemed to be up-to-date on all the latest news on Dahmer's confinement in prison, his trial, and certainly the dark deeds he perpetrated.

"Good reading?" I'd asked and it caused Emory to jump and let out a little cry of alarm.

I sat down beside him and pulled out a tuna salad sandwich from a brown paper bag. "Sorry, didn't mean to scare you."

Emory turned the newspaper over so the story about Dahmer wasn't face up. "It's okay," he said.

We ate in silence for a few minutes, and then I asked, "Any new stuff on him?"

"Well—" Emory slouched back in his seat, and I could tell he was ready to talk. He was always ready to talk about Dahmer. It was freaky, but it made Emory more interesting than 99 percent of the folks who work here. "There's nothing new to me. As you know, I've been following his case ever since it first was in the paper last July." He shut his eyes, and I had to imagine he was recalling—and maybe relishing—hearing the first details right after Dahmer got caught last summer. "But there's stuff here the public might not be aware of."

"Like what?" I asked.

"Like how he almost got caught after killing one of his first victims."

"Really? How long ago was that?" I asked, thinking that this must have been a fairly recent development, within the past five years anyway, in Milwaukee—or shiver—even here in Chicago. But Emory surprised me.

"He was only eighteen. So was his victim, a guy named Steven Hicks." Emory went on to tell me all the gruesome details, how he bludgeoned the poor guy with a dumbbell after a night of drinking at Dahmer's parents' house in Ohio. He then strangled him with that same dumbbell. Later, he dissected and dissolved the body with acid.

"Sick." I pushed my half-eaten sandwich away.

"Wanna hear the kicker?"

I wasn't sure I did, but I nodded anyway. "Dahmer got pulled over by the cops with the guy in a trash bag in his car. He told him he was just going to the dump. They believed him. Can you imagine?"

Well, in retrospect, it seemed like a horrible lapse in judgment, but at the time, in small-town Ohio, a local patrolman might not jump to the conclusion that some *kid was driving around with a dead body in a plastic garbage bag. Really. Would you jump to murder and dismemberment first thing?*

"Wow. If they'd stopped him back then, looked inside the bag, they might have prevented who knows how many deaths?"

"At least fifteen," Emory said softly. "Although I know there were more."

"Why do you think he did it?"

That was always the big question.

Emory looked at me for a long time, and I could tell from the concentration on his face that he knew the answer or at least thought he did. "He wanted him, just like all the others, to stay with him."

I nodded. I'd read that too. That his killing victims, and even eating parts of them, was a way of keeping them with him.

"There are better ways," I said, pointing out what I thought was the obvious.

"Maybe he didn't see things through your sane and rational eyes," Emory replied.

I was weirdly complimented. And the fact that I thought so made me think I might have some of the same weirdness as Emory.

He's just fascinated by all of this because he's lonely. And hurting. *I thought. That was all it always boiled down to, which is why I never felt repelled by Emory, who despite his fascination with Dahmer, seemed so sweet, so desperate for human connection. He lived alone in his apartment near Loyola, his sister having pretty much abandoned him after his mom passed.*

It was this last thought that made me throw out a proposition. I knew he was not only lonely and alone, but poor. It was hard for him to make ends meet, though somehow, he was keeping his head barely above water.

"Hey, what are you doing tonight?"

Emory grinned, but there was no joy, no mirth in it. "Same old, same old. Home. Lean Cuisine. A little TV and then bed. Get up and start it all over again in the morning."

I shoved the remains of my lunch back in the sack and offered, "Why don't I come home with you? We can order a pizza from Giordano's and maybe check out what's on offer at Blockbuster. Something gory."

"I don't know," Emory said, but I could tell he was tempted.

"Come on. You just said you had literally nothing to do tonight."

And he'd agreed. And their pizza and horror movie night were born.

It was a weird way to fall in love with a guy. But that's what happened, Tyler thought, God help me.

He started down the rows of cubicles, pausing only to check to see if Emory was at his desk. He was, with his headset on.

Tyler would wait to talk to him.

Before sitting at his workstation, Tyler paused to take a final look out the window. He could see the gothic spires of the Tribune tower, and beyond that, the dull gray waters of Lake Michigan. Under today's cloudy, windswept skies, the lake looked lethal, arctic. Tyler could imagine an iceberg floating in toward the city from the horizon.

He sat and put on his headset, but he couldn't begin work just yet. He was still thinking of Emory, of how tonight, Tuesday, would be their horror movie and pizza night.

Of all the guys Tyler had been with, and there'd been a few since he'd lost his virginity in the basement men's room of the campus library when he was a freshman, he'd never been so cautious, so circumspect, so, really, shy around another man.

It was the signals Emory gave off. Conflicting. On the one hand, his loneliness and need for human connection emerged out of him like some sort of aroma, like liquor seeping out of a drinker's pores. And yet, he managed to keep Tyler at arm's length, even now, months after they'd met and months after his mom had passed away.

It was like he was both attracted to and repelled by Tyler's interest.

And Tyler himself was confused by why he bothered. Was it because he was attracted to Emory? That much was certainly true. Although, at first glance, Emory was eminently forgettable. His ashy complexion, mouse-brown hair, and hooded eyes would never make him stand out in a crowd, let alone a gay bar. But look closer and you'd find something deeply sexual about him—in a nerdy sort of way. Tyler fought conflicting desires to hold him, kiss him, rip his clothes off, criticize those same tired LL Bean wannabes from Kmart, walk away from him, and to finally make him look in a mirror, just so Emory could see the appeal he had—the broad shoulders, the trim physique, the little gap in his front teeth that made Tyler want to stare at that mouth for hours. His lips were thick, and Tyler could imagine losing himself in them, their salty sweetness.

He'd never felt like this about a man in all of his young life. He'd experienced lust, of course, but Emory brought out something more. A kind of moth-to-the-flame charge that was all the sexier and more alluring because Emory had no idea he possessed it.

A part of Tyler, the part he sometimes thought of as the sane part, knew he should move away from Emory. He should be choosing to head out with people his own age, cruise the gay bars, enjoy life and playing the wide-open field as a young man in his twenties should...and could. He should be fighting off hangovers, fielding phone calls from suitors, making the most of his youth and beauty. Gather ye rosebuds... Tyler had been good in his survey of English lit class.

But no. Like a mule, he was stubborn in his attraction and now was merely, or so he told himself, waiting for it to bear fruit.

He pulled out the top sheet from the list of calls he would need to make that day—a million-dollar request for life insurance from an attorney who lived in Kenilworth.

Chapter Nine

Emory stopped in his tracks when he heard Tyler calling him.

"Hey, hey! Are we still getting together tonight?"

Emory turned, already bundled into his down coat, muffler, knit cap, and mittens for the L ride home. He squinted at Tyler, his blond, bland innocence.

"I'm sorry. Did we have plans?" Emory simply wanted to make the journey to Edgewater, shedding the day and the crowds of smelly commuters behind.

He wanted to see if there was another missive from Jeffrey Dahmer waiting in his mailbox, wanted the time to open the envelope slowly and to relish how special he felt being a sort of confidante for Dahmer.

Tyler laughed. Emory watched as a blush rose to his cheeks. "Yeah, we did," Tyler said. "Come on, Emory. It's a thing now—our Tuesday nights. Pizza, stuffed spinach pie, and a horror movie from Blockbuster on Broadway. We've done it for a couple of weeks."

There was such hope in his face that Emory could hardly bear to extinguish it with a no. Still, he liked being alone. He had too many secrets these days to risk spilling them to someone else.

Anyway, while he was most certainly alone, he wasn't lonely. He visualized the stack of letters, now numbering in the dozens, arranged neatly on his desk, from the very first one back in July to the most recent one, only two days ago.

At the very least, Emory needed to get home to hide the letters. There were certain things he could share with Tyler, including letting him know he corresponded with Dahmer in prison, but he could never reveal the depths of their closeness and how much Dahmer relied on Emory to, at last, be the one man who "stayed."

Emory attempted what he hoped would pass for a grin. "Oh yeah, yup. You are right again, Mr. Kay." Emory tossed Tyler a bone. "We were going to see if they had *The Exorcist III*, right?"

"Right! The Gemini killer. They were out of it last week."

Emory moved closer to Tyler. "I'm on board, my friend. But you need to give me an hour or two to run some errands and clean up the place before you come by. Is that okay?" Emory knew it wasn't. Why should it be? Tyler lived in the suburbs. It would make no sense for him to go home and then return to the city when he could just accompany Emory back to his apartment on Kenmore Avenue.

Tyler's face fell. He shrugged. "I guess I could go have a drink somewhere."

"Good idea! Tell you what—I'll pick up the pizza. My treat. If you could swing by the video store and grab the movie, we'll be all set. Come over around seven?"

Tyler nodded, unsmiling. "Sure."

Emory, rare for him, reached out and squeezed Tyler's shoulder. "Good man." He turned and hurried toward the elevator, knowing Tyler wouldn't be able to follow because he hadn't yet suited up for the frigid temperatures outside.

*

At home, Emory paused in the vestibule of his building with a sense of anticipation that nearly stole his breath away. His hands were trembling as he opened the mailbox.

There it is.

The only missive in the mailbox—a letter from Dahmer. No return address, but Emory had grown accustomed to the handwriting, the slight backward slant, the mix of cursive and lettering. The black ink. He held it for just a moment, weighing it to see if he could determine, before opening, how many pages might be inside. He felt like a kid on Christmas morning, shaking a brightly wrapped mystery box.

Just behind him, one of his neighbors came in, sighing with relief at the meager warmth in the vestibule and stomping the snow off her boots. It was Nancy Chefalo, an older woman who lived on the seventh floor. She was always friendly, despite him never offering her any encouragement. He found her red lipstick too lurid and her dyed-black bob just a pathetic attempt to look younger when in fact all it did was make her wizened face appear paler and older. Maybe someday he could tell her, under the guise of being a well-intentioned friend, why she should simply let her hair go natural and to wear less makeup. *She may think she looks thirty, but she looks every bit of sixty...or even older.*

"Hello, Emory!" she cried breezily, as though they were old friends. "Cold enough for you?"

"Good afternoon," Emory replied, separating the key to the front door from the others on his ring. He turned his back to her, but it didn't stop her from leaning in to peer over his shoulder. Emory clutched his letter close to his chest, feeling affronted.

She was too fast for him. "A handwritten letter from someone, huh? You must be pretty special. Those damn things are rarer than hen's teeth these days, aren't they? I mean, all *I* get is junk and bills!" Emory unlocked the door to the sound of Nancy emptying her own mailbox and sputtering, "Yup. Yup. Same old. Same old. They should put a trash can out so we can just dump this crap right here."

"Good idea," Emory said.

She followed him inside the open door, gesturing at the envelope he still held close to his chest, as though protecting it. "From an admirer? A pen pal?"

"You could say that." Emory hurried away from the woman, but she matched him, step for step, on his way to the twin elevators at the opposite end of the lobby.

"Must be nice. Is it from a girl? Or a boy?" She giggled. "I don't judge."

Heat rose to Emory's cheeks. *What does she know?* "It's from—" Emory's voice trailed off. *Wouldn't she be stunned if I told her? Maybe she'd finally keep herself to herself.* "It's from, um, none of your business."

She actually made a little yip sound, as though he'd pinched her, that coincided with the chime of the elevator doors sliding open.

She didn't utter another word on the way up, for which Emory was grateful.

In his apartment (and it still felt weird thinking of this space as *his*, when it had once belonged to his family), Emory shed his outer garments and threw his backpack on the couch. The radiators under the windows began to clang and hiss, and Emory took the comforting noise and promise of heat as a welcome.

He plopped down at his desk and, taking up the silver-plated dagger opener his mother once used, slit the envelope down the side and pulled the single sheet of lined notebook paper from it with all the care of a forensics specialist.

This one was short, much to Emory's disappointment. But in its sparse array of words jumbled on the page, it managed to say a lot.

Emory,

Thanks for the update. I'm glad you're moving on from your mom's death. She'll always be with you.

Emory drew in a quivering breath and felt an immediate and hot sting of tears at the corners of his eyes. For the briefest of moments, he imagined Mother's touch on his shoulder. It seemed so real, he glanced up from the letter, almost expecting to see her standing next to him.

Thanks for letting me know about this guy in your life. Tyler, is it? Congrats that he likes you. I hope you'll make the most of this one and won't let it end up like that body in the alley from last summer.

You were lucky to get away with that one.

This one, be more careful. Keep your business private. It's what I did. And I know it failed me in the end, but look at how many years I was able to do what I did, and no one knew, Emory. People are stupid! Even when the smell of decomposition was stinking up the hallway of my apartment building, folks complained to the landlord about rotting hamburger! Jesus Christ.

No. Enjoy your time with Tyler. And if that time is enjoyable enough, he'll stay.

Jeff

Emory set the letter with all the others he'd gotten from Dahmer over the past few months. There was now an impressive stack of them on his desk, and once more, he counted them. With this one, there were now an even twenty letters from him.

Emory believed there was no one else in this entire country who could claim to have the relationship he did with Dahmer. He should write a book! He shook his head at the mere idea of it though. That would be a betrayal. Here, Dahmer had chosen him out of what Emory was sure were many admirers and sickos, to be the person he advised, to whom he turned to for support when the going got rough—as it certainly must in prison.

That he cared about Emory and his life felt like some kind of achievement. And achievements, in Emory's bland and boring life, were few and far between.

He wished he had time to write back, but it would have to wait. He only had an hour or so before Tyler would show up on his doorstep, ringing the annoying buzzer to be let in. And, in that hour, he needed to shower and to call Giordano's to order a pizza for delivery, even though he could scarcely afford the splurge.

He'd write after Tyler left. Sometimes, when he wrote just before falling asleep, he would dream of Dahmer. The dreams were never frightening or aggressive, but usually romantic, with Dahmer holding him close, running fingers through Emory's hair and teasing him with butterfly kisses on his cheek. Sometimes, they got a bit more graphic than that, and Emory would awaken with the inside of his Jockey briefs sticky.

For now, he simply took the stack of letters and slid them into his desk's top drawer. They were the only things in there. And it was the only drawer in the desk that he kept locked.

He undressed quickly in his bedroom and stood for a moment before the full-length mirror he'd helped himself to from Mary Helen's nearly empty bedroom after she was gone. He had a full-on erection and knew it was because Dahmer had showed him attention. As he always did, he reassured himself there was nothing sick about this response. It was natural, right?

He watched himself as he stroked, watched until his seed shot out of him, arcing out to land on the gritty hardwood floor at his feet.

And then he lowered himself down on all fours and licked his semen up, eyes shut and imagining it was Dahmer's.

*

When he opened the door to Tyler, Emory was more relaxed and in control. He wore a pair of faded Levi's with a red Wisconsin Badgers hoodie he'd picked up at the thrift store on Halsted, the Brown Elephant.

He smiled, actually glad to see Tyler because he now knew Dahmer approved of their relationship, maybe even encouraged it. Opening the door wider, he stepped aside so Tyler could enter. "Pizza should be here any minute now."

"Great. Let me give you a few bucks toward it, okay?"

Emory shook his head and closed the door behind Tyler. "Don't insult me." He pointed to the black plastic bag in Tyler's hand. "Did they have it?" he asked hopefully.

"Oh yeah, they did." Tyler brought out two blue-and-white Blockbuster boxes. "*Exorcist III* and a surprise." He grinned.

"What is it?"

"Oh, it's one I'm pretty sure you've already seen, but it holds up under repeated viewings." Tyler stuffed the videotapes back into the bag. "It's a surprise." Tyler set the bag down on one of the shelves of the pale-oak entertainment unit that dominated the living room.

Tyler eyed him. "You look great. Two things I find very sexy on a man—bare feet and damp just-out-of-the-shower hair."

Emory let the comment hang in the air for a second, debating whether to acknowledge it. In the end, he said, "Get out of your coat and stuff." Emory attempted to keep the irritation out of his voice. Tyler's coat and boots were dripping on the floor, which was dirty enough without mud stains.

Tyler began taking off his outer garments. When he was down to the khakis and pale-blue button-down he'd worn to work, he crossed the living room and moved into the dining room, where he could hang his winter stuff over a dining room chair.

"They're still dripping," Emory whispered. He went to the kitchen to get a tea towel to clean up the mess.

"Sorry about that." Tyler squatted down and pulled the towel from Emory's hand. "Let me do that. I brought the mess in." And he quickly sopped up the puddle. The coat and muffler had at last stopped dripping.

And Emory was on the floor, on his knees, face-to-face with Tyler. It was a simple moment, but a heart-stopping one. Something hung in the air. Was it anticipation? Fear? Lust? All of the above? Emory placed a hand over his gut. Something fluttered inside.

"The pizza will be here in a jiffy," Emory mumbled. "Should we queue up the movie?"

Tyler cocked his head and his face lit up with a sly grin. Emory noticed, maybe for the first time, how intensely blue Tyler's eyes were, but a deep blue unlike run-of-the-mill irises. "Your eyes are freaky."

"I get the dark blue from my grandma. Hers were almost a cobalt."

Emory was on the verge of telling him his eyes were beautiful, but quickly censored himself, holding the compliment in check. Men didn't tell other men they had beautiful eyes.

"You like them?" Tyler finally asked, his voice a little hoarse.

Emory wanted to get up from the floor but was rooted here. He thought of Dahmer's words—*Enjoy your time with Tyler. And if that time is enjoyable enough, he'll stay.* Would it be so awful if he reached over, right now, and touched his cheek, still rosy from the cold? Would it be sinful to simply lean forward and kiss those full lips, silently begging for a touch?

Emory licked his own lips, finding them as dry as his throat and his mouth's interior. He didn't have to wonder anymore what to do because Tyler decided for him. He leaned in and very gently brushed his lips across Emory's. He went back on his haunches and looked at him, the mischief on his face making him even more attractive. And then he leaned in again, pressing his lips with even more force into Emory's own. When he slipped his tongue into Emory's mouth, Emory surprised himself. He didn't resist. And even though he'd just gotten himself off less than an hour ago, he was ready to go again.

Everything came crashing to a halt, though, when the buzzer sounded. The loud mechanical bark, an intrusion, caused Emory to gasp and pull away from Tyler as though he were on fire. He leapt to his feet.

From his position on the floor, Tyler peered up at him.

Flustered, Emory said, "Pizza must be here. Hungry?"

Tyler nodded. And Emory didn't know how to respond to the playful look in those deep-blue eyes. He turned quickly and headed to the intercom to quiet the buzzer, which was now sounding again. He pressed a button to admit whomever was downstairs without bothering to ask.

In a minute, there was a knock on the door.

Emory hurried to it, imagining Mary Helen and her girlfriend standing out there. The minute he opened the door and saw what Emory knew was his flushed face and Tyler kneeling on the hardwood floor, they'd know what was going on. Know and be delighted. And Emory couldn't abide the idea.

But it was only the pizza delivery guy. He was dark-skinned, with wavy black hair spilling out of a Cubs baseball cap and sparse facial hair.

He looked down at the ticket stapled to the top of the box and then back up at Emory. "Stuffed spinach?"

"That's me." He groped in his back pocket for his wallet and felt a pang of alarm when there was nothing there. He turned, mouth open, to find Tyler standing next to him.

"You dropped this." Tyler handed him his worn leather wallet. "You sure you don't want a few bucks?"

Emory waved him away and then pulled money from his wallet, enough for the pizza and a generous tip.

"Queue up the movie," he told Tyler. "I'll get plates." And he left him to go into the kitchen to lay out the Fiestaware, the knives and forks. He yanked a couple paper towels off the roll for napkins. The smell of tomato sauce, garlic, basil, mozzarella, and spinach were barely contained by the box. Normally, the aromas would have Emory's mouth watering, but tonight, they didn't have the same effect.

He was hungry, all right, but it wasn't for pizza.

*

Later, after they'd worked their way through the entire pizza (somehow, Emory found his appetite) and watched both *The Exorcist III* and *The Texas Chainsaw Massacre*, they lay together on the couch, in front of the TV. The credits still rolled, and the dark screen managed to throw a flickering light on Tyler's face.

Emory had to admit he liked the feel and the warmth of Tyler's body next to his. During the second movie, Tyler wrapped his arms around Emory and tucked himself into him, laying his head on his shoulder. Normally, Emory might have been appalled or at least in shock if another man did this to him, especially right here in his own home, where he still felt Mother watching, looking down from a celestial perch.

But he was, surprisingly—and most of all, to himself—at ease.

"It's late," Emory said.

"That it is." Tyler reached over to the coffee table and snagged the TV remote and the one for the VCR and switched both off. The room was lit now by a weird blue light pouring in from the windows. The moon outside was bright. Or maybe it was the night sky, grayish white because of yet another snowfall on the way.

Whatever it was, Emory didn't want to move, didn't want to break this fragile moment. It was the first time since Mother had died that Emory didn't feel so alone, so isolated.

He knew Tyler would leave soon, to get home at even an indecent hour. He already felt an empty place in his chest, an acute longing. And Tyler had yet to stir from his place on the couch, let alone make a move toward the door.

The obvious didn't occur to Emory.

It did to Tyler though. He lifted his voice up to penetrate the dark. "I could stay, you know."

Emory tightened involuntarily. He hoped Tyler didn't notice his sudden intake of breath, his shoulders rising up and stiffening. It was a big line to cross. In the end, all he could do was ask, "Really?"

Tyler stood and his figure was a black silhouette, backlit by the bluish light streaming in from the living room windows. The view emphasized that Tyler was a man, not a boy. His shoulders, in this light, were broad. Emory realized for the first time that Tyler was over six feet tall.

He wanted desperately to pull him back on the couch, to yank him down on top of himself. But he couldn't. He was paralyzed.

Emory was certain Tyler sensed his desire and his hesitation because he took Emory's hand, using it as leverage to pull him up and off the couch. Emory was unsteady on his feet and stumbled against Tyler, which made Tyler wrap his arms around him to steady him.

"Yes, really. Let's go to bed. We can clean up in the morning."

Emory stood close, smelling him, the clean, pure animal scent of him. "I should throw out the pizza box and rinse off these plates. They'll attract roaches."

"Let 'em feast. I've been waiting since last summer to get you into bed, and tonight seems to have conspired to make my dream come true." Tyler met his gaze despite the wan light. He turned and stooped a little as he looked outside. "It's begun snowing. I doubt if I could get home even if I wanted to. And I don't." He kissed Emory again. "Come on." He tugged on Emory's hand, already knowing the way. "If we're lucky, the snow won't stop. We'll have a blizzard. And we'll get a snow day tomorrow."

Emory followed. He paused only long enough to glance out the window, at the cone of big, fluffy white flakes pouring down, highlighted by the streetlight just outside the window.

Was he dreaming?

Or was this a dream come true?

Even though it was Emory's own apartment, he allowed Tyler to lead him to the bedroom. He stood still, breathing heavily, eyes squeezed shut, as Tyler slowly removed his clothing. When Tyler was done, he sucked in a breath and ran his fingertips lightly over Emory's chest.

And then he pushed Emory down on the bed.

Emory simply lay there, still, unsure of what to do.

He could hear Tyler undressing, the soft snick of his zipper being lowered, the clatter of his belt as it hit the hardwood floor. And then... And then, he almost cried out as he felt the bed being weighed down as Tyler climbed on.

Emory thought he should be doing something. Saying something. Even moaning, as the guys did in the porn movies he sometimes watched at the adult bookstore up on Howard Street. But he felt frozen to the bed, unable to move. There wasn't enough spit left in his dry mouth to speak, let alone do anything else.

Other than sleazy bookstore encounters, which almost seemed unreal to Emory, like something that had happened to another person, this time was truly his first. Not just with a man. With anyone. He couldn't move for fear he'd do something wrong. He was terrified Tyler would laugh at him. Or, worse, run out of the apartment when he realized exactly how inexperienced Emory was.

After all, Emory was old enough that it was embarrassing that this should be his first time. Didn't most guys have their first times in their teens? He wanted to tell Tyler, so he would go slow, be gentle, maybe even instructive. Paradoxically, he was desperate that Tyler not recognize his lack of experience.

Hence, the laying here, the immobility, the terror of even opening his eyes.

It's not your first time, idiot. What about the guys you let fuck you at the bookstore? They don't count? It was Mary Helen's voice he heard.

Tyler rolled toward him, and Emory felt the silk of his skin as he climbed on top, their bodies fused together full length. The weight was crushing, but Emory wouldn't have stopped Tyler for anything.

The next thing he knew, Tyler was kissing him—hard, his tongue thrust into Emory's mouth. The kisses burned. And the pale stubble on Tyler's face, almost invisible normally, was sandpapery against Emory's skin. That sensation made his dick twitch.

After a while, Tyler pulled back. There was a pause in the room that went on too long. Finally, Tyler asked, "Are you enjoying this?"

Emory forced himself to open his eyes. He peered up at Tyler's face, only inches away. Even in the darkness, he saw the concern and maybe even confusion in his eyes, the way his features furrowed. He reached up, so he could feel Tyler's stubble beneath his fingertips.

Emory pulled his hand away. "Why would you ask that?"

Tyler's lips flickered in a brief smile. "Um, because you don't seem to be enjoying yourself. I just want to be sure I'm making you happy."

Emory wanted to reply that what Tyler was making him feel was something beyond happiness. Maybe joy. Elation? A feeling of completeness? But it was as though he couldn't get his lips and tongue to work together to form so much as a single word.

"Am I?" Tyler asked again.

Emory lifted his head and saw Tyler's flagging erection.

No. I can't do anything right. What do I say? What do I do? In the end, Emory was able to find his voice, even though it came out whispery, squeaky. "Maybe we could just cuddle?"

Tyler said nothing for a moment. Then he got up and pulled the bed clothes out from under Emory. "Sure. It'll be cozy here under the blankets with you." He pulled the blankets and top sheet down to the foot of the bed so Emory could move up and put his head on the pillow. Then he lay beside him, nestling himself into the crook of Emory's armpit and pulling Emory's arm around him.

"I'm a loser," Emory whispered.

"What?" Tyler got up on one elbow.

"Nothing."

Tyler slid from the bed and moved across the room. Emory was certain the next thing he'd do was put on his clothes and beat a hasty retreat. And that caused a longing deep in Emory's heart. "Where are you going?" he asked, mournful, certain he already knew.

Why would anyone want to be with me?

"Just to do this." Tyler moved to the window and yanked the shade up to the top. The room was flooded with a pale-blue light from the moon's luminance and the snow coming down.

It was beautiful.

Tyler got back in bed with Emory, pulling the covers up to their necks, and snuggling close.

Emory wanted to weep. He knew he wouldn't sleep, but that was okay.

Yet he did sleep and, at some point during the night, he felt Tyler, pressed close to his back, slip inside him. It hurt, and Emory sucked in a breath but didn't tell him to stop. He gripped the pillow tighter and waited for Tyler to finish, worried that he wasn't using a rubber.

In the morning, the room was flooded with brilliant light from the sun in a cloudless blue sky and from the reflective illumination on the mounds and mounds of snow that had fallen as they slept.

Emory looked around the room, as though Tyler could be crouching behind his chest of drawers. "Tyler?" He sat up and felt a throbbing dull pain in his ass, which let him know he hadn't dreamed what had taken place.

He pulled the covers back, praying that there wouldn't be blood or worse on the sheets.

Everything was clean.

"Tyler?"

But there was no answer.

Chapter Ten

Tyler couldn't do it.

He'd thought Emory would be someone he could get close to, someone he could love and care for. He even thought he could be the person to bring Emory back to some kind of semblance of life. Emory had hidden depths and, once upon a time, that was part of his appeal.

Now those hidden depths weirded him out and, frankly, terrified him.

Emory was unlike anyone he'd ever known. His oddness was, rather than repellant, magnetic. Tyler saw aligning himself with the man as the key to assuming his place in the adult world. None of his friends from school, none of the guys he'd dated or even hooked up with, were anything like Emory.

And that was a plus.

He thought he and Emory might have a quirky relationship, insular. Emory and him against the world. He imagined long weekends holed up in Emory's apartment, cooking or ordering takeout, watching old horror movies that were at once terrifying and Mystery Science Theater hilarious.

Last night, things had gone as he hoped, better than he dreamed and then, along about three a.m., everything changed.

Tyler remembered waking and feeling several odd sensations. The first was that the bedsheets beneath him were soaked. There was a sour smell in the air. Tyler didn't want to have to decide if the odor was sweat or piss.

He turned to tell Emory about his discomfort, if maybe there was another bed they could move to.

But Emory was gone. The bed was empty.

In the odd blue light of the moon, Tyler sat up. Emory was absent from the bed but was still in the room. Tyler sucked in a breath as his gaze moved to the corner where there was one of the chairs from the dining room table.

Emory sat naked on it, eyes closed. His erection poked up between his spread thighs. His naked form almost glowed, spectrally white, in the wan light.

What might have been sexy was decidedly not.

Emory whispered to himself, very rapidly. At first, Tyler could make out none of the words. Slowly, as though there were a wild animal in the room baring its teeth, Tyler slid back down on the damp sheets, much as he didn't want to. He half closed his eyes, hoping that Emory, if he did open his own eyes, would think Tyler was still asleep.

Tyler watched, alert, listening. At first, only a few words came to him, "Mother" being one of them, repeated over and over. He said something like "I'm a good boy, Mother. I'm not like that."

Tyler's eyes adjusted to the dim illumination, and as he made that adjustment, he began to understand more and more of what was emerging from Emory's mouth, his fevered whispers.

"Jeff. Jeff, I know what you want. I know what you need. I'm the only one. I'm the only one." Emory swallowed and then went on. "I'd stay with you. No question. I'd be yours."

He whispered these words like a prayer, a litany, and Tyler felt goose bumps rising on his skin. Suddenly the room felt a lot colder than he knew it actually was. One of the main things Emory had talked about since Tyler had met him the previous summer was his fascination with the serial killer from Milwaukee. Tyler shrugged it off. He himself had his own fascination with serial killers and had done his fair share of reading about them, especially if there was a gay angle to their cruelty, their obsessions. On his bookshelf at home, there were true-crime books about John Wayne Gacy and Larry Eyler, both from Chicago, and Dean Corll, from Texas. Between the three of them, those men had killed possibly close to a hundred young men. And now Dahmer had joined their ranks.

Tyler understood Emory's fascination and had viewed it as simply the same kind of thing as his passion for horror movies. Creepy, but not out of the realm of the normal.

Tonight, though, Emory's whispers to "Jeff" as though he knew Dahmer personally, had been too much. It demonstrated to Tyler that Emory didn't just have a morbid curiosity about the dark side of human nature but was too close to that dark side himself.

The thought sickened Tyler and made him doubt his own judgment.

Tyler had lain frozen in that position for a good, long time, a half hour at least. He'd become so stiff, his muscles ached.

When at last Emory returned to the bed, Tyler made a sleepy grunt, and rolled over, away from him.

He lay staring at the wall until Emory let out a loud, bloodcurdling scream, and then went silent, his breath that of someone in a deep sleep. He shook a few times, as though in the throes of a seizure.

Trembling, heart pounding, Tyler forced himself to slide from the bed. He stood and tried to steady himself, staring down at Emory's slumbering form. His mouth was dry; he almost couldn't swallow. The thing that really made him shake his head, aside from his terror, was that only a couple of hours ago they'd made love. Not fucked but made love. It had been quiet and quick. But Tyler was sure he'd experienced a deeper intimacy than he ever had. Apart from Emory being passive, it had been good, a sign that even more was on its way.

This was a start.

Tyler had fallen asleep spooning with Emory, imagining scrambled eggs, coffee, buttered toast, and golden sunlight when the morning came.

And now he saw Emory as insane, someone to fear. Tyler hated himself for it even though he knew he had every reason for his feelings.

He dressed quietly and quickly. He considered a shower to wash the sweat, if it *was* sweat, off. But he feared waking Emory and, suddenly, even though it was still dark outside, he wanted out of here.

He tiptoed through the bedroom and then headed across the living room toward the door. He paused in his tracks and nearly shrieked when he heard Emory's voice behind him.

"Where are *you* going?" There was an accusation in the question.

Tyler swallowed hard and turned. His mind was blank. He could think of no response. He simply stared at Emory.

And as he did, Emory laughed. "I get you. I should have known you wouldn't stay. He understands that. He understands *me*. That was always his gripe—they never stay."

Tyler had a hunch. "Are you awake?"

Emory's stare was dead, projected at a fixed point just above Tyler's head. Tyler wasn't even sure Emory knew who he was talking to. His question, apt as it was, might have been just a coincidence.

For a long while, neither moved.

Then Emory turned and disappeared into the shadows of his bedroom.

Tyler hurried out the door, Emory's soft laughter behind him.

*

Now, he stood in the vestibule of Emory's building, looking out. Because it was winter, dawn's grayish light would not arrive for a couple more hours. The snow had stopped, and pristine mounds of the stuff lay untouched on the sidewalks.

There were few cars on the street this early in the morning. When one did pass, it threw up a spray of snow, its headlights illuminating the banks that had fallen during the night.

Tyler tightened his scarf and, taking a deep breath and bracing himself, stepped out into the dark.

In spite of the biting cold, exacerbated by the wind rushing off the lake just a couple blocks to the east, Tyler felt better outside; there was a sense of relief and liberation. He stood still for a moment, simply breathing in the bracing air and watching it emerge from his mouth as a cloud of steam.

He looked back through the doorway to the lobby, almost expecting to see Emory behind him. But not even a doorman stood watch.

What do I do with myself now?

Tyler looked up and down Kenmore Avenue, deserted for once. It was too late to go home and too early to go in to work. He wished there *was* time to get back up to Wilmette, so he could change clothes and shower. He wondered if he reeked from the damp bed he'd lain in.

It was a small problem compared to what he'd just seen. He shook his head. *What did I see anyway?* He wasn't sure he could believe his own eyes, his own memory.

It's one thing to think someone's quirky and odd in a delightful sort of way. It's quite another to see their delusions, and yes, their sanity laid bare. The image of Emory sitting naked and erect in that chair, mumbling not only to himself, but also to a serial killer, plagued him. Tyler didn't know if he could purge it from his brain, even though it was already taking on the eerie shimmer of a dream.

Or a nightmare.

Tyler turned south and walked to the corner, his footfalls crunching as he made tracks in the newly fallen snow. At Granville, he made a left and, despite the arctic wind blowing his way, he trudged the few blocks over to Lake Michigan.

He ended up at the beach at the end of Thorndale Avenue. The traffic on Sheridan Road had picked up as the morning commute began. Behind him, the flow of cars sounded like the rush of water. He sat on a bench, shivering. The waters raged, the waves flinging themselves restlessly on the beach. He could imagine he was at the ocean.

In the east, the sky was beginning to lighten. The illumination was barely perceptible at this point, just a thin line of lavender at the horizon. Still, it was beautiful. Tyler felt reconnected to the world in a way.

Once upon a time, he'd met a boy, and his name was Emory Hughes. They'd worked together. They'd watched movies—they loved the same ones. And they'd even shared one another's bodies in a moonlit bedroom.

It should have been good. But it was a detour away from real life, Tyler realized now. He was a young man, barely into his twenties. He shouldn't be holing up and hiding away with a disturbed, lonely man. It was all right to feel sorry for Emory, to even show him a bit of kindness and affection, because Tyler knew, from his limited view into Emory's world, he was sorely in need of those qualities.

But being considerate of a fellow human being, Tyler realized, didn't have to be at his own expense.

He stood. It was just too damn cold! When he turned, he saw the north side of the city spread out before him, just coming to life—lights on in apartments, the L stop at Granville housing a stopped but rumbling southbound Red Line train, a few people picking their way through the still untouched snow.

He began making his own way toward the L station.

He'd made two decisions—one, he'd head downtown and linger over a big breakfast, pancakes, bacon, coffee, at the diner near the building where he worked. And two, when he got home tonight, he'd call up some of his old friends, the ones he'd ignored since starting his job last summer, and see if they wanted to head down to Halsted for a few drinks.

And maybe he'd meet a nice boy.

One who didn't mumble in a dark corner to the world's most infamous serial killer.

Chapter Eleven

Dear Jeff,

It's been a week since Mother's life insurance came through.

It wasn't much, certainly not enough to live on for a long time, but adequate to keep me for a few months, maybe even as long as a year while I figure out what to do with my life. Good thing the payment came through, too, because guess what? I quit my job! No more bitchy bosses, no more smelly, crowded L train cars, no more hours of mindless work, benefiting no one except an overly rich insurance company. No more being a prisoner in a cubicle hell.

I didn't really mean to quit...at least not so suddenly. It was sort of an accident.

I told you about Tyler abandoning me in my last letter. When I woke and he was gone, I was devastated. I thought we'd started something beautiful the night before. I thought he was my soul mate. I thought we'd be together forever. I thought the union of our bodies meant something.

It was that day I quit my job even though I didn't know then I was quitting.

I couldn't go in and face seeing him after he left me lying alone in the bed we'd shared without even so much as a goodbye. I spent the day moping around the apartment, remembering how he'd promised to make us breakfast in the morning and how we might turn the day into a snow day, like back when we were schoolboys.

I waited around, thinking he might return. Maybe he was out, picking up coffee, I told myself.

I looked for a note.

When the hours passed and the sun came streaming in, I knew he wasn't coming back.

Ever.

I tried calling him at work a couple of times. It's hard enough to get through to someone who makes his living on the phone, harder still when you're pretty sure that someone wants nothing to do with you.

I didn't report off that day, nor the next. Finally, on the fourth day of my not turning up, Jennifer Vidovic, my boss called, whining at me. Why hadn't I called? Did I realize how irresponsible I was being? What was the story?

The story, bitch, is that I was fed up. I'd had enough of eight hours of mind-numbing boredom every day, of mindlessly repeating the same words, over and over, to different people. Sick of writing up reports with boilerplate words.

I felt like a puppet with no brain of my own.

"I'll pack up your things and send them to you," she said, very curtly, before hanging up.

And, just like that, I was free.

I've spent the past seven days thinking about Tyler, about what I should do. It's hard to just let him go. Especially now, when it seems I have no one.

Emory

*

ONE WEEK LATER.

Dear Emory,

It's good you found your way out of the boredom of the work world you were in. I had a bunch of jobs, and none of them ever gave me any kind of satisfaction. Heck, not even working in a candy factory was any fun. I can't stand chocolate to this day.

You'll be okay. You've got some money now, and that will buy you time. In here, I realize now what a precious commodity time is.

And Tyler? He doesn't know what he's missing. I can tell from the letters you write me that you're intelligent and kind. That you have a soul. If I was out, maybe you and I would have met one fine night, long ago. And a lot more disappointing men would still be walking around.

But we'd be together, Emory. Because you're the only man in the world who understands me.

What might have been are the saddest four words in the English language.

I know I'll never be free. But I have some words of advice for you about this Tyler person. You seem to care very deeply for him, maybe even love him.

So don't give up.

Be there for him.

Let him know that you care.

If there was a spark there before, you can rekindle it.

Love,

Jeff

*

Emory stared at the letter. He'd never signed it with *love* before. It gave Emory's heart a little jolt. Could he and Jeffrey Dahmer have been a couple? The thought repelled and caused a shiver to crawl up his spine. But Emory would be lying if he said there wasn't some thrill mixed in with the chill.

And what he'd said about Tyler? Emory shrugged. He wasn't sure if he should let him go, or simply try again. Emory had never had a real relationship with anyone before, much to his shame. He didn't know how these things worked—what the difference between pursuing someone versus stalking them.

It occurred to him that Tyler looked very similar to Dahmer, and he wondered why he'd never noticed before, caught up as he was in the sensational story of Dahmer's apprehension and dark story.

There are ways of reaching out to Tyler.

As he was pondering what he should do, the buzzer sounded.

Emory jumped, startled. The sound of the buzzer had become so rare he had to think about what it was for a second. It was like a metallic bark, and Emory felt it like a cold jolt to his bowels.

He moved to the window that overlooked Kenmore, but the awning prevented him from seeing who was out there.

Maybe it's Tyler? Maybe he's come to apologize, to beg for my forgiveness?

Emory glanced at the clock on the VCR. *No, it's midafternoon. Tyler would be and should be at work.* Still, Emory himself had left behind the monotony of those cubicles and endless forms, maybe Tyler had done the same, inspired. *Perhaps that's what he's coming to tell me? Sure, I bet that's it.*

A burst of joy lit up his heart like the sunlight filtering through Mother's red glass vase on the windowsill. He rushed to calm the buzzer, which was ringing now repeatedly. For so long, the whole Hughes family hadn't been able to utilize the two-way function of the intercom.

Over the years, what was once audible was so garbled as to be useless, so they simply shrugged and buzzed whoever was downstairs in.

Which is what Emory did now—certain Tyler was coming to call.

After pressing the buzzer, he waited by the front door.

There were two sharp raps. Breathless, Emory swung the door open and felt the hope and expectation fade from his face like a cloud's shadow wipes out the sun.

"Expecting someone?" Mary Helen stood in the hallway, shifting her weight from one foot to the other. She looked different. Her spiky hair had grown out a bit and now lay, a little greasy, flat against her scalp. The dye she used was only visible now at the tips of her hair. Her real color, a mousy brown, was back in full force. She was bundled up inside a red down-filled coat.

"Why would you ask that?"

She brushed by him and kicked the door closed behind her. "Because you looked so disappointed. For Christ's sake, your dear sister, whom you haven't seen in a month or so, drops by and you look horrified." Mary Helen laughed.

She moved into the living room and plopped down on the couch. She surveyed the mess, her lips turning up in a grimace, her nose twitching with distaste. "What the hell's going on here, Em?"

"What do you mean?"

She threw up her hands. "What do I mean? Look around! This place is a mess."

It was true. The coffee table was crowded with Styrofoam cartons from the diner on Granville and pizza boxes. Crumbs lay scattered across the table's surface. Emory had left his soiled clothes in heaps on the floor, on one of the side chairs. He didn't know what to say. "I wasn't expecting company," seemed absurd.

When did he give himself permission to live like this?

"Struck mute, huh?" A bitter laugh escaped her. "And it stinks. What is that? Piss?"

Emory shivered. "No, no. Of course not." He denied it but was unsure himself. He'd smelled nothing until she brought it up and now, a sour ammonia smell permeated the air. Emory felt his face heat up with embarrassment.

Exasperated, he asked, "Why are you here, anyway?"

Mary Helen eyed him. Her features softened in the wan winter sunlight filtering in through the Venetian blinds' slats. Emory felt a jolt of horror as he realized: *she feels sorry for me. She pities me.*

Mary Helen, voice usually marred by sarcasm, came out softer. "You're my brother, Emory. I know we haven't been close recently, but I do care about you." Her gaze roamed over the room once more. "Are you okay? I called your work, and they said you quit."

Emory nodded. "That's right. I couldn't take it anymore. That place was sucking the life out of me, stealing my soul."

"It always did sound like a horrible job; I'll give you that."

"And with Mother's life insurance coming through, I thought I could take some time and figure out what I wanted to do with the rest of my life."

Mary Helen stood and began picking up his abandoned clothes and tucking them under her arm. "That makes sense, Em. It really does. But that money? It's not gonna last long. And you're shouldering the rent and all the bills on this place." She moved into the bedroom where Emory presumed she was putting the dirty clothes she picked up into his wicker hamper.

She came back and started picking up the food containers, the glasses, and the dirty plates. Emory shuddered as a couple of cockroaches scattered off the table and scampered off into the space between the floor and baseboard. He was tempted to stop her from cleaning for him but was unable to move from his perch on this hard chair at the side of the room.

He stayed quiet and listened as she took out the garbage to toss it in the dumpster outside. Remained rooted to his seat as water ran in the kitchen. Mary Helen said nothing as she washed dishes and stacked them on the counter.

When she returned, she eyed him, hands on her hips. "I helped you out a little here. But the place still stinks." She rubbed the toe of her boot into the floor, peering down, then looked back up at him. "The floors are filthy. I don't even want to think about the bathroom or the sheets on your bed." She sat back down on the edge of the couch close to him. Emory flinched when she laid a hand on his knee. "Listen. Listen."

Emory looked at his sister and couldn't believe what he saw—tears in her eyes. He didn't think the bitch was capable.

"Hear me, bud. You're not well. I can see that. I don't know what to do." She cocked her head. "You wanna come and stay with Liz and me for a bit? Maybe this place is too much for you."

And that last remark made him mad. "Too much for me? It wasn't too much for me when I had *two* full-time jobs, one downtown and the other here, playing caregiver to our mother because you couldn't be bothered. Why would it suddenly be 'too much for me' now? Huh?" He waved her away and lurched back so that her hand dropped from his knee.

Mary Helen's mouth dropped open. Maybe because Emory had never before stood up to her. The tears remained in her eyes. A couple ran down her face. She wiped them away with the back of her hand. "I'm sorry. I should have been around more for you. I was mixed up, not sure where my own life was headed. But that doesn't excuse anything." She sighed and her gaze moved to the sunlight filtering in and illuminating the dust motes dancing in the air. "Let me help you. Let me make it up to you."

Emory realized suddenly, and chillingly, that there was no way she could ever *make it up to him*. Too much dirty water had flowed under the bridge of their sibling relationship. Too much trust broken. Too much care damaged.

Emory stood and walked to the door. Inside his head, a nest of hornets swarmed. But he felt preternaturally calm, almost numb, as he opened the door and stood there with it swung wide, his hand on the knob. "Thank you for cleaning up. It's a good start. I promise to mop the floors, give the toilet and tub a good scrubbing, and do a massive load of laundry downstairs. But I need you to go now." He opened the door a little wider. "I appreciate your concern." He stared at a point above Mary Helen's head, unable to meet her eyes. Those tears were too much.

"Wow." Mary Helen got up from the couch to cross the room. She stopped in front of him and said nothing until he at last looked into her eyes. "You call me, okay? You need anything, you change your mind about coming over to stay, you call me."

She laid her hand on his cheek, and he winced, drawing back.

She shook her head.

"The loss is just sinking in, huh?"

"I don't know what you're talking about," Emory managed to say, the words coming out borne on a strangled breath. He wouldn't cry in front of Mary Helen. He stared down at the floor, not wanting to look in his sister's eyes anymore. They were too much like Mother's.

"Okay." She edged by him.

Emory wondered if he'd ever see her again. He watched as she walked slowly down the hallway toward the elevator, her head bowed and shoulders hunched.

As she stood in front of the metallic doors, she turned and looked back at him. When her eyes met his, something passed between them, something Emory couldn't describe, but which he knew he felt as closure. She gave him a little smile. Pathetic.

He went back inside without waiting to see her board the elevator.

Part Three

Spring

Chapter Twelve

At the end of March, the most amazing day presented itself—a glimmer of what was to come after the long, dark, and icy winter.

It wasn't until afternoon, though, that Emory first realized it, immersed as he was in his morning routine, which now consisted of 150 sit-ups, 200 push-ups, and jumping jacks for twenty minutes. Thank God, there were no neighbors downstairs.

After his exercise, he had what he called an ascetic's breakfast, which consisted of a soft-boiled egg over dry toast and a cup of black coffee.

He would then read the newspaper with the intention of finding a job in the classifieds, but really to search for news about Jeff. There hadn't been much, since he'd been sentenced to fifteen consecutive life sentences on February fifteenth. In his statement to the court, Jeff's words, so sad and regretful, chilled Emory.

"I should have stayed with God," the *Tribune* quoted him. "I tried and failed and created a holocaust."

It was a jab to Emory's heart when Jeff said, "I didn't ever want freedom. Frankly, I wanted death for myself. This was a case to tell the world that I did what I did not for reasons of hate. I hated no one. I knew I was sick or evil, or both. Now I believe I was sick."

That day in February, just after Valentine's Day, was a day that broke Emory's heart because he knew that what he'd thought all along about the killer was true—he didn't want to do what he'd done. He'd been driven by forces outside himself that compelled him, irresistibly, to do what he'd mightily resisted.

Emory hadn't heard from Dahmer since he'd been sentenced even though he wrote to him every day. Each day, Emory approached the mailbox in the building's vestibule with the hope of a dreamer. And each day, as he rifled through the solicitations and the bills with no satisfaction, he'd mumble, "Maybe tomorrow."

The poor man had been sentenced to fifteen consecutive life sentences, so the possibility of parole, and ever seeing freedom again, was off the table. No wonder he wasn't up to writing.

Emory would be here for him when he was ready.

Emory had faith that the day would come. Somehow, someone besides himself would see the truth behind the crimes of Jeffrey Dahmer.

Would today be the day he'd finally get a letter?

After his breakfast, Emory would clean the apartment, top to bottom. He scrubbed floors and toilets, took out the garbage from the day before, washed and dried his dishes, glasses, cups, flatware, and pots and pans. He made his bed even though no one had seen the place since Mary Helen had dropped by last winter. The apartment smelled of ammonia, bleach, and Murphy's soap.

The floors shone. The windows sparkled. The cockroaches had even beat a retreat, feeling starved out by Emory's relentless cleaning and the boric acid he sprinkled behind appliances and along the baseboards.

His fingers were raw and red from all the work and all the detergents. His nails were bitten to the quick.

He showered three, sometimes four times a day.

He'd shaved his head and most of his body, to keep it clean, to remain pure.

So it wasn't all that surprising that when he looked up, a little after his lunch of brown rice and kidney beans, that the day outside his windows looked summery, even though it was March, not a typically warm time for Chicago. Emory had expected to see gray skies, maybe raindrops on the glass. Lord, maybe even snow flurries.

Emory lingered on the view outside his windows, with its endless blue skies, broken up by a few puffy clouds high up. Because it was a Saturday, the kids were out of school and out in force along the sidewalks of Edgewater, playing hopscotch, jump rope, hide-and-seek, and riding bikes. Their voices carried, even though Emory's windows were closed against winter's chill.

He opened them now.

The warm air that wafted in was a shock. Even the breeze had lost its undercurrent of chill. It honestly felt more like June than March.

Emory had been promising himself he'd begin a running regimen as soon as the weather got warm enough for it to be bearable along the lakefront trails.

No time like the present, Emory told himself. His weight had dropped over the winter, but he liked being skinny and seeing his ribs. It made him feel clean, like his body was an efficient tool, burning away all his fat reserves until what remained was a pristine machine, glorious.

He thought of Tyler often and wondered what he was doing, if he still worked downtown at their mutual once-upon-a-time place of employment.

In his darkest hours, he imagined Tyler in the arms of another man. The nasty images that rose up made Emory run to the bathroom and puke up whatever meager food he'd consumed. He had to force thoughts of Tyler away as much as possible. But here was the conundrum—the harder he tried *not* to think of Tyler, the more he did.

Emory went into his room and dug out a pair of old gray sweatpants and a long-sleeved T-shirt. Even though the sun's brilliance promised balmy temperatures, he knew that along Lake Michigan it would still be chilly. That huge body of roiling blue/gray water held ice in its makeup, and Emory knew it would be more than happy to share that coldness with him.

Once his running shoes were laced up and tied, he set out.

*

Night.

Emory was restless. He found he couldn't sit still—not to read, not to watch TV, not to eat, and certainly not to be alone with his own thoughts.

He'd had so little contact with *anyone* over the past few months. He needed to get out, if not to mingle with people, to at least be among them.

Jeff had once told him that he needed this interaction, this rubbing shoulders and elbows with his fellow humans. It was natural. People were designed to connect. Emory didn't quite understand why Jeff held this view since the serial killer seemed to hate most folks, himself in particular. But maybe he was trying to make Emory a better person than he was. Perhaps he recognized a kind of salvation through improving Emory's lot since it was now much too late to better his own.

So, Emory showered and dressed. He was ready to go out around nine o'clock, a time when he'd normally slide between his flannel sheets.

He took a look at himself in the mirror hanging on the back of his closet door. At first, he jumped, because there Mother stood behind him in the mirror. Her head cocked, she smiled. Love, rather than sickness, radiated from her eyes. She reached out a hand, as though to smooth his hair or brush a stray piece of lint off his shoulder.

But when he whirled around, fully expecting her to be there even though his rational mind was screaming that it couldn't be so, the empty room mocked him. When he turned back to the silver glass again, only his own reflection looked back.

Seeing now through Mother's eyes, he barely recognized himself. When he'd quit his job last winter, he was a completely different person. He had a spare tire around his waist. His hair was a dingy shade of mouse brown. His shoulders, hunched, told a tale of a person who wanted to be invisible.

Now, though, in his button-fly Levi's and heather gray T-shirt, he was transformed. He stood tall, accentuating his much leaner frame. The shaving of his head made his eyes appear larger, more luminescent. The shearing of hair, rather than making him appear a victim of male-pattern baldness, gave him a more manly, confident look—as though he were telling the world he was comfortable and confident in his own skin.

Even if he wasn't.

Mother had always said to act the part and the part would become you.

He pulled a blue fleece jacket from the closet because, once the sun went down, March chill had risen back up, accompanied by a misty precipitation that shrouded the streets outside in fog, creating halos around the light from the streetlamps.

Spring was always a flighty, fickle bitch.

He avoided the elevator and hurried down the flight of stairs that would take him to the lobby. Once there, he paused in the vestibule, pacing for a moment outside the banks of silver metal mailboxes that lined one wall. Of course, he'd checked the mail earlier, on his way back from his run, in fact. And all that was in the mailbox was the usual blend of solicitations and demands for money.

No letter from Jeff. Just like every day...

But something, a pleading little voice, told him to check the mailbox one more time. He'd never known there to be a second mail delivery before, but he felt compelled to grope for his keys and then use the one that would open the mailbox's little door.

Inside, there was a letter.

He pulled it out cautiously, as though it were flammable, and gasped when he saw it was from Jeffrey.

Going out would have to wait. Emory turned on his heel and rushed back upstairs.

Once in the apartment, he switched on the brass table lamp next to the couch and plopped down with the missive. With trembling hands, he tore the envelope open.

Dear Emory,

Almost a month has passed now since my sentencing. It's unreal to imagine that I now have to give up five consecutive lifetimes to pay for my crimes. Even cats have only nine lives. Where am I going to get five to pay for what I did?

Not your worry, my friend. Not your worry.

I know I'll be here for the remainder of my days, however long that turns out to be. The worst part is not the sentence, or that I will never again know what it's like to simply be free, to go to a grocery store and buy food, to see a movie at the local show, to sit on a bar stool and have a beer.

Life, as I once knew it, is over.

I can accept that. What I can't accept is the shadow of fear that dogs me now.

The other guys in here? Every one of them hates me with a passion even I, the infamous and depraved serial killer, can't imagine.

Emory, one day they will kill me. Mark my words.

I just don't want it to hurt. I look forward to escaping this world, but I don't want to have to go in terror and in pain.

You're thinking, and rightly so, I dispatched my own victims with terror and pain accompanying them. But that's not true. I tried to be kind to them, even as I was killing them. I always wanted their deaths to be kind of soft surrenders, a giving up of the suit of clothes they wore as men, releasing their spirits.

Does that sound too woo-woo spiritual for you? It was true.

I hope none of the men I loved (and I loved every one of them, even as the life ebbed out of them while they were in my arms) suffered.

You have to live for me, Emory. Be the man I always wanted to be. A man who loves himself first so others can love him back.

Get Tyler back.

Keep him with you.

Jeff

Emory stared down at the scrawled handwriting, the scratched-out words, the blot of ink that perhaps was made by a fallen tear. It was one of the clearest letters Jeff had ever written him as well as one of the longest. Emory worried about him, alone in his cell, afraid that someone would take something sharp to him, or worse, beat him to death with fists. Maybe he'd be strangled after being raped. Maybe the latter had already happened.

Emory put his head against the back of the couch.

There was nothing he could do for Jeff in prison. Maybe someday, if he could get up the nerve, he'd visit him there. It wasn't all that far away. And he was sure Jeff would put him on an approved visitor's list if there was a need for it.

But for now, he needed only to do what Jeff had asked: *live for him.* And, Emory hastened to think, *live for myself.*

He'd make sure Tyler knew, without a doubt, there was no other man that could love him as Emory could. No one would adore him more.

Eyes shut, he allowed himself a brief imagining—Tyler curled up beside him on this very couch, the flickering light of an old horror movie, something like *The Last House on the Left*, flickering over the both of them. Spilled popcorn on the couch, their skin just touching.

Bed later, awakening in the other's arms, the sheets warm from the sun and their own bodies. Breakfast in the morning.

A whole life together.

He opened his eyes at last and stood.

What does the night hold?

*

As he was walking to the Granville L stop, he passed the Forge as the door to the bar opened. On a wave of stale beer and smoke, a pair of younger guys, their arms wrapped around each other, staggered out, laughing. "Hey, you wanna three-way?" one of them called to Emory, which caused them to laugh even harder.

Emory tried to peer into the bar before the door slammed shut again, but all he saw were shadows. He shivered as he thought of the bartender who was murdered the night he was last in here (the only time he'd ever been in the Forge) and wondered why that night remained a large black and blank spot in his memory.

Did I kill him? Could I have?

He knew he probably had, in a bizarre sort of homage to Dahmer, in a supreme act of self-loathing. But yet, there was the uncertainty. If only he could remember...

He paused and watched the two young men, one with a shaved head like Emory's own and the other a redhead with a big gut and a beard, head east, toward the lakefront. One of them, he guessed, had an apartment in one of those high-rises lining Sheridan Road.

He shook his head to free it from the pornographic images that arose. They fled once the pair rounded the corner on Sheridan, headed south.

What do I care what they get up to?

Tonight, he would brave the Saturday night crowds on Halsted and go to one of the busiest establishments along the strip, Sidetrack. He'd never been, but he'd heard it was some sort of video bar, with screens all over the place. From what he'd read in one of the gay rags, they showed all sorts of stuff—old TV sitcoms, Broadway musicals, maybe even softcore porn. The notion of this last option caused a kind of weird queasiness to rise in his gut—delightful and paradoxically revolting, all at the same time.

Emory didn't know how interested he was in watching anything, but he figured the screens would give him a place to focus his gaze. He'd be alone, but he'd be doing *something*. He could be out among people without being too obvious, he thought, as he slouched against a wall, with a bottle of beer clutched in his hand.

He wanted to be part of a crowd.

He also wanted to be invisible.

During the walk from the Addison stop, he nearly changed his mind several times. He got a lot of stares, mostly from the gay men he encountered in the busy Wrigleyville neighborhood, some even swiveling their heads to take him in approaching and walking away. He wasn't flattered. All the attention did was to make his face burn.

Was he suddenly visible, maybe even attractive?

He shook his head. *Impossible.*

*

Sidetrack was packed. Emory stood for a moment, frozen, in the doorway, just before the guy on a stool, checking IDs. He didn't move until someone behind him called, "Dude. You going in?"

Emory turned to look at a kid, really. If he was even in his early twenties, Emory would have been surprised. He had black hair and eyes to match. He used those eyes to shoot impatient daggers. "Goin' in or what? Tonight would be nice."

"Give me a second, please. Just getting my wallet." Emory moved forward, his driver's license out for the doorman's inspection with the flashlight he held.

The doorman ran the beam of the flashlight over Emory's ID and handed it back without even a glance at his face.

Emory walked the few steps it took to get inside the bar proper.

Even though the main room of Sidetrack was crowded with wall-to-wall people, Emory had never felt more alone in his life. Despite speakers blaring dialogue from a sitcom and the voices in the room shouting to be heard overtop the canned laughter, the party atmosphere was lost on Emory. Truly, he was a stranger in a strange land.

You're here now, a voice in the back of his mind told him, a voice that sounded much like what he imagined Jeffrey Dahmer to sound like, *you might as well make the best of it. Who knows? Maybe if you ease up just a little and quit being so self-conscious you might even enjoy yourself.*

"Oh, what do you know?" Emory said aloud, earning him a look from a bespectacled guy standing near the entrance, sipping something red from a martini glass. A little swirl of lemon peel moved in the drink like a fish.

"What?" he asked. A little smile played about his lips as if he were missing out on whatever joke he was supposed to get.

"Oh, nothing," Emory said. "I was just thinking out loud."

"Sounded more like you were arguing with someone." He raised his eyebrows above the rims of the little round gold frames of his glasses. And then he grinned, and in that grin, Emory found comfort.

He's not laughing at you. Say something.

Emory pointed to the guy's glass. "What's that you're drinking?"

He glanced at his glass, which prompted him to take a sip. "It's something new. Called a Cosmopolitan."

Gravely, Emory nodded. "What's in it?"

"Damned if I know. Fairy dust, snips and snails, and puppy dog tails." He laughed. "I *can* tell you there's vodka and cranberry for sure." He took another sip. "Maybe lime or lemon?" He drained the glass and peered at it curiously. "Guess it's time for another." He cocked his head and Emory thought, for a moment, that he would offer to buy him one. "You should try one."

He walked away and left Emory in a sea of people, where he imagined himself as some kind of buoy, bobbing on drunken waters.

Emory moved along the side of the bar, keeping close to the wall. He found a corner where no one stood and took up his place there. The only problem was he'd have to give it up to go get a drink. By the time he came back, the spot would undoubtedly be gone.

Emory was never much of a drinker anyway. He'd just stand here and watch, see what the natives did. Maybe he'd learn something.

A clip from the old TV sitcom *Maude* came on, and it caught Emory's attention, not because he'd loved the show (even though he would admit, if only to himself, that he knew every word of the theme song), but because it released a memory. His mother, long before she was sick, belonged to a Tuesday night bowling league, and while she was out at the Head Pin, over on Broadway, he'd babysit Mary Helen. They'd loll on the living room floor and watch TV until Mother came home, often sharing a box of powdered sugar doughnuts, which they'd dunk into mugs of milk. They'd stay up, in their pajamas, until Mother came home, usually around the time the news made its ten o'clock appearance.

"Nice to see you smile."

The voice drew him out of his reverie, and he had to refocus away from one of the big monitors above him to see who'd spoken.

When he did, his mouth dropped open. "Tyler?"

It was like waking from a dream.

But there he was, standing right in front of him, holding a tall glass of what Emory assumed was vodka and tonic. It looked refreshing, bubbling, with a lime wedge floating on the surface.

Tyler smiled broader. "In the flesh."

He looked no different. The same blond hair, a lock of which now fell over his forehead, obscuring part of his left eye. He may have even gained a bit of weight—he seemed stockier and more substantial. His grin melted Emory's heart. Until this moment, Emory hadn't realized how much he'd missed him even though he'd thought of him almost every day over the past few months.

Emory mumbled, "You look good."

"Thanks. And you? Emory...you've really changed. I almost didn't recognize you. But then I saw that telltale faraway look in your eyes, and I said, 'That's my old friend.'"

Emory didn't know whether he was happy or sad to be described as a friend. On the one hand, "He still thinks of me as a friend," and on the other, "*Only* a friend." *How do I reconcile?*

"Yeah, it's me," Emory said.

"You look good, man. Slimmed down...and mean!" Tyler laughed, but in a sexy way. "Did you find another job?"

Emory shook his head. "Nah. I'm either overqualified or underqualified for everything, seems like. You still at Quality?"

"Nope. Got out of there shortly after you left." Tyler grinned. "I got an editor gig at one of the magazines at the American Medical Association over on Grand Avenue."

"You like it?"

Tyler shrugged, took a sip of his drink. "It's a little boring, honestly. But it pays pretty well, and I have my own office, so that's cool."

Emory didn't know what to say. He glanced down at the floor, noticing the cigarette butts and the grit. When he looked up, Tyler had moved a few steps away. "It was nice seeing you, Emory. I got to get back to my friend."

"Okay." Emory watched him walk away, disappearing into the crowd and then re-emerging near the bar. A big guy in a green-and-black-flannel shirt with a stubbly beard and a buzz cut grabbed Tyler and squeezed him, planting a peck on his lips.

As he did it, a wave of laughter erupted in the place in response to a clip from *America's Funniest Home Videos*, but it felt to Emory as though they were laughing at him.

For being such a fool.

Of course, he has someone else. What did you expect? Him to stay alone, pining for you? Don't make me piss myself laughing. The voice in Emory's head was Mary Helen's.

He watched as Emory and the big guy, a bear as they called them, leaned against the bar and turned their attention to the screen, their gazes cast upward. The bear had a bottle of Budweiser clenched in his meaty paw, and it seemed like he couldn't get it down fast enough. His other arm was thrown casually, maybe even possessively, over Tyler's shoulder. Tyler didn't mind, in fact, he leaned into the man.

A nest of hornets, unleashed, buzzing, in his brain. The hot acid of bile splashing against the back of his throat made him grimace. *Is this jealousy? Is this what it feels like? I thought it was much more benign.* He turned away from the view, but all that he could look at were taunting, laughing faces that reminded him of the movie *Carrie*. He could hear Piper Laurie, as Carrie's mother, in his head, warning, "They're all gonna laugh at you."

Emory worried that if he had telekinetic abilities right now, this whole damn bar could go up in a glorious cloud of flame, shooting up toward the ink-stained heavens. *Laugh at me indeed!*

The crowd closing in was a crushing weight. His breathing came more rapidly, and he panicked, wondering if it would continue coming at all. He rushed from the bar.

Outside, the cold night air was a shock, but one he appreciated. Even though the air was perfumed with car exhaust and an undercurrent of Lake Michigan's water beneath the fumes, it was pure heaven to draw it deep into his lungs. The kaleidoscope of streetlights and car headlights merged, and Emory felt drunk as he wandered north on Halsted, even though not a single drop of alcohol had passed his lips. The crowds on the sidewalk, mostly gay men, some costumed in leather, a couple flamboyant ones in drag, and the rest just average Joes pressed up against him, almost as they had in the bar.

He wanted to get away, to get home, to his sanctuary and his shelter.

The claustrophobia rose, making his blood boil, causing his heart to constrict, reducing his breathing to the pants of a dog on a hot and humid August afternoon.

Emory leaned against a brick wall outside a bar at the corner of Cornelia and Halsted called Little Jim's. He closed his eyes, wondering why he hadn't just stayed home, especially when he knew how busy Halsted would be on a Saturday night. Behind his closed eyelids, he saw first shooting colors—blue, purple, aqua. And then a ghostly image of his mother, her hands outstretched.

I don't belong here. I never did.

After he got his heart rate and respiration back to somewhat normal levels, he hurried into Little Jim's, thinking maybe a coke or even a beer might calm his nerves before he headed back home on the L.

But he paused in the doorway, because it was just as crowded in this bar as it had been in Sidetrack, although the crowd here was one-hundred percent male. *Don't gay men do anything besides drink and cruise each other?* The smoke, too, made him cough. There was a blue-gray cloud of the stuff hovering near the ceiling.

When he glanced up at one of the TV monitors hanging over the bar, he winced, because it was showing hardcore pornography. A young blond was in a sling, being gang fucked by a group of men...and not one of them wore a condom. The vision actually made him tremble, made him feel like, once again, he was about to be sick.

He turned and fled, running all the way to the Addison L stop.

Dorothy had it right. *There's no place like home.*

All the way back north, all Emory could do was stare down at the floor where someone had spit out the hulls of sunflower seeds.

Chapter Thirteen

"Is everything okay?" Cole tried to catch Tyler's gaze. It seemed, over the course of the last fifteen minutes or so, all the spark had gone out of his friend. When Cole had picked him up earlier at his new studio apartment near Lincoln Square in the Ravenswood neighborhood, Tyler was bouncing off the walls so much that Cole wondered, "What are you *on*?" He'd seen enough of his friends indulge, especially the gay ones, in what they all merrily called nose candy through the eighties and into the nineties. And he'd seen the more hardcore ones end up in rehab, their lives lost to dealers, and the worst of them, their lives lost, period.

But Tyler had just said, "I'm excited to be going out, that's all. High on life and all that happy horseshit." Tyler grinned and it made Cole realize just how much he was falling for this guy, who wasn't his type at all. But there was something about him—his exuberance, his utter lack of judgment, his kindness, and, of course, the tightest little butt this side of the Mississippi.

He didn't know if Tyler returned his feelings, but as the evening started out and they walked together through an alley running under the L tracks to the stop at Western Avenue, he'd begun to think maybe he stood a chance with Tyler even if he was ten years older and a good deal meatier than what he'd noticed Tyler seemed interested in when they were out.

They'd met only a couple of weeks ago, at the gay bowling league at the Marigold Bowl. Tyler had been there to cheer on a team where he'd had several buddies. But he was *not*, he'd told Cole over beers and after the league bowling was over, a bowler. "Maybe if I made aiming for the gutter a priority, I might knock over a few pins." He'd rolled his eyes. "Reverse logic, you know?"

They'd been inseparable the past couple of weeks, and many of Cole's friends thought they were a couple, but the truth was the most intimate thing they'd done so far was to share a pizza while watching a video Tyler had brought over of *Carnival of Souls*. Cole hadn't confessed his hatred of the horror genre, because he wanted Tyler to like him. But at some point, he'd need to clear that up and confess that his love for movies fell within the opposite realm—romantic comedies and chick flicks. Despite being almost six-and-a-half feet tall and well over two hundred pounds, he was a softie at heart. A Hallmark commercial could make him blubber. He couldn't help it if he looked and sounded like a long-haul truck driver, but at his core, was a delicate flower, prone to tears and hearts-and-flowers romance.

And the delicate flower side of him picked up on Tyler's change of mood almost immediately. It was right after he crossed the bar to talk to a frightened-looking fellow with a shaved head.

Now, Cole leaned close to whisper in Tyler's ear. "You seem, I dunno, kind of disoriented, like you lost your best friend."

Tyler looked at him with wide eyes. "Are you reading my mind? That guy I was talking to? His name is Emory and maybe he was my best friend, or something like it, but there were issues. I haven't seen him in a long time, and seeing him now, kind of shocked me."

"Why?"

"He looked, I don't know, so severe. Kind of off." Tyler thought for a moment, a finger to his lower lip. "I hurt for him."

Cole took a swig of his beer, but it suddenly had no taste. If Tyler hurt, then so did he. "Why would you hurt for him?"

Tyler looked down at the floor and then back up at Cole. The laughter all around them suddenly seemed out of place, maybe even a little macabre. Tyler shrugged, but the light had vanished from his eyes.

"Do you want to get out of here? Go someplace quieter?"

That pulled a smile from Tyler's worried face. "Are you propositioning me?"

If Cole thought for a moment that Tyler's answer would be yes to a proposition, he would have even jokingly said he was. But Tyler was obviously disturbed, and Cole wanted to be a support, not a lech, so he grinned and shrugged. "No. Just want to know you're okay."

Tyler leaned into him and placed a hand on his chest. "You're sweet. You're one of the sweetest men I've met in a long time."

Cole responded with, "That's what they all say." And it was true; it was both Cole's blessing and his curse that guys, for the most part, didn't look at him with lust, but with the kind of emotion one might reserve for a beloved uncle, dad, or grandpa. He was sweet. He was kind. But sexy? It didn't seem to cross many minds. And he really wished it would cross Tyler's.

"Thank you. I think you are too."

Cole's words didn't seem to register on Tyler, which made him even sadder.

And what Tyler said next ruined the whole evening for Cole.

"I do want to get out of here, but would you mind if I took off on my own?"

"Really? We were having such a good time."

"It's not about that." Tyler eyed him with sympathy. "Or you. I just need to see if my friend is okay."

Cole tried to comfort himself with the notion that this, right here, was ample demonstration that Tyler was a good, caring person.

He should like that—and he did—he really did, despite his disappointment. He should save that disappointment, though, for another time.

It wasn't easy to do. "Sure. Go to your friend."

Tyler was already moving away. Cole reached out and grabbed the back of his jean jacket. "Call me in the morning, okay? Let me know how things go."

Tyler nodded and started to exit the bar once more. But he stopped himself, hurried back to Cole, and kissed him. It wasn't a peck either. There was a little flicker of tongue before he pulled away.

And that made Cole smile, even though he was looking at Tyler's back as he weaved his way through the crowd and toward the exit. Cole wanted to do a happy dance but contented himself with ordering another beer.

Chapter Fourteen

During the day, the Edgewater neighborhood where Emory lived was okay—safe, normal. The sidewalks bustled. Shops, restaurants, and bars served crowds. There was something alive in the air. Tyler bet most of the people on the busy daytime streets never thought much about crime, about dark shadows lurking in alleyways or the rustle of rats in the dumpsters.

Night changed everything.

Now, at nearly midnight, the streets were silent, save for the swarm of traffic on Broadway that sounded to Tyler like a rushing river. And yes, there was the occasional rumble of the L just a block east of the busy thoroughfare. But neither of these things made Tyler feel any less alone. Neither of these mechanical sounds comforted him or gave him confidence. He still looked over his shoulder every few paces.

He stopped outside Emory's building. There was a streetlight just above the long front awning, and it was out, making the darkness here more palpable. Tyler shivered as he imagined a man in a black ski mask separating himself from the shadows and approaching him with a gun, a knife, or murderous outstretched hands.

He looked up at the high-rise, hoping for a glimpse of stars above the rooftop. But noise pollution rendered any constellations or planets invisible. Even the moon hid behind a cloud bank, discernible only from a faint pewter light.

Does he even live here anymore? How's he paying the rent if he isn't working? Is he awake? These were just a few of the questions running through his mind, making him hesitate, and causing him to question if following after Emory had been a foolish idea, given the late hour of the night.

But it wasn't really so much that the wee hours of the morning were beginning, it was the memory of the last time he'd seen Emory before tonight, whispering to himself in a corner filled with shadows. That scene, etched on his brain, seemed like something from one of the horror films he favored, although with a movie, he always had the comfort of *this isn't really happening. There are cameras, a boom microphone perhaps, a director and a crew pulling the strings of terror. It's all make-believe. Keep telling yourself, "It's only a movie. It's only a movie."*

The very *real* image of a madman was what had driven him away last winter.

So why are you here now? The guy's nuttier than a fruitcake, as Grandma used to say even though she'd never met Emory. What do you hope to get out of this little encounter if you do happen to talk to Emory?

Tyler walked a bit north on Kenmore, glancing into dark underground parking garages, and asking himself again: *Do I really want to do this?* His life these days was good. Free of drama. The life of a carefree twentysomething. He had a decent job that challenged him—the work was dull, but editing soothed him in a way, ensuring that no mistakes slipped through was a badge of honor for him.

He'd made new friends even as he lost touch with the old ones from high school and college.

All part of growing up, he supposed.

But he now had a core group of young gay men like himself, who enjoyed getting together and going out to the bars on Halsted and sometimes up in the Andersonville neighborhood, seeing movies on the weekends, just hanging out with a six-pack and a bong at each other's places. Laughing. Teasing. Comparing notes on *boys*.

There were hookups and one-night stands. No one guy ever amounted to much.

He didn't have anyone special although he knew Cole had a serious crush on him. But he wasn't sure he wanted that, so he didn't let it show that he knew, let alone return the interest. He was a sweet guy, but Tyler had yet to feel that indescribable spark for him.

And he'd felt that spark, albeit in the tiniest way, for Emory, a few months ago. His oddness had extinguished the spark, but not his concern for Emory.

Tyler was a nurturer, had always been. Growing up, his mom confided in him, even if it wasn't appropriate. He welcomed being a kid-sized shoulder to cry on. He'd listened patiently as his mom described her dreams of another life or complained how her husband didn't 'see' her anymore, how she was taken for granted, little more than a glorified maid.

And he worried about Emory. Seeing him tonight had been a shock. He reminded him of Travis Bickle, the character Robert De Niro had played in *Taxi Driver*, especially after Bickle had shaved his head and gone full-bore crazy. "You lookin' at me?" Tyler could still picture the iconic scene in the mirror from the film.

Was Emory in danger of going over the edge?

Tyler turned back around and headed for the front door of Emory's building. He needed to not only make sure Emory was all right, but also to let him know there was someone there for him, someone who cared.

It was the least Tyler could do.

He walked up to the intercom to the right of the front door, found Emory's name, thankfully, on the directory, and buzzed him.

There was no response to the buzz, so Tyler pushed the button again, leaning a bit longer this time on the button.

Still...nothing.

He jabbed at the button a few times, knowing it was useless, and then turned to walk away. He bet he could find Cole still down on Halsted. And if not Cole, a Mr. Right Now, to round out his evening in at least a physically satisfying way. He shrugged. It was the way of the world, how his life really was these days.

As he neared the end of the awning and the sidewalk proper, he heard the click of a door behind him. He turned quickly, thinking maybe he could slip inside and try knocking on Emory's door.

But it was Emory himself who stood there, a silhouette backlit by the light in the lobby behind him. "What are you doing here?" Emory's voice rode out, ghostly, on the damp night air.

Tyler froze. *What am I doing here, anyway? Do I really need to see this guy again? Do I want to make myself vulnerable?* The answer to his questions must have been a yes because Tyler lifted his lips in his most concerned smile and started back toward Emory.

"I was on my way home." Tyler moved close to Emory, until they were face-to-face. "No. That's a lie. I wasn't 'in the neighborhood and thought I'd stop by.' When I saw you at Sidetrack, it made me worry." Tyler searched Emory's eyes for some sign of understanding, but his face stayed slack, impassive. He crossed his arms over his chest.

"Worry? Why?"

Tyler shivered. He cocked his head a little. "Do you think maybe I could come in? It's chilly out here."

Emory glanced into the lobby behind him, as though someone might be lurking there, watching them. But it was empty. Still, the hesitation prompted him to ask, "You're alone, right?"

That made Emory smile, but it was bitter. And the smile didn't rise to meet his eyes. His gaze was as dead a shark's.

Are you sure you want to go inside?

"Always alone. Naturally." The bitter smile stayed put.

Tyler was torn. *Should I just admit this was a mistake, turn around and head for the L?* He acknowledged this course of action would be a relief. But then a better, more nurturing part of himself spoke to him. *Or should I be the friend I came here to be?*

In the end, he decided to be a friend. "You seemed so different when I saw you. It made me remember our good times together, Emory. It made me think back to our horrible work at Quality Investigations. It made me think of our movie nights." Tyler smiled and felt the heat of a blush rise to his cheeks. "It made me think of a lot of things." He shrugged. "I guess I'm just concerned for you and wanted to see if you were okay."

"At almost one o'clock in the morning?"

"Is it that late?"

"Yes."

Tyler stood with him for a minute or two of painful and awkward silence. "Please. Let me come up." He grinned. "I'll keep my hands to myself."

That made Emory laugh. He stepped aside so Tyler could come in. He led him to the utility stairs at the back of the building to go up.

Once they were in the apartment, Tyler was stunned at the change. The living room, dining room, and the partial glimpse into Emory's bedroom revealed a kind a Spartan cleanliness. The floors looked scrubbed and had a dull sheen from the single illuminated floor lamp in the living room corner. The air had a scent of Murphy's Oil Soap to it. There wasn't a thing out of place.

Other than the cleanliness of the place, only one thing had changed. Now, above Emory's desk against a wall in the dining room, there was a cork board. On it were newspaper clippings. Lots and lots of clippings.

Every single one of them was about Jeffrey Dahmer. The headlines jumped out at Tyler, ghoulish, turning his stomach.

Body Parts Litter Apartment.

Grisly Anatomy of a Crime.

Dahmer Sane.

Little Body Shop of Horrors.

Face of a Madman who Killed 17 and Ate Them.

They gave Tyler a chill more intense than anything he felt in the damp outdoors.

Emory noticed him looking. "I keep up with how things are going. For him."

Tyler eyed him. "They sent him away forever, right?"

Emory nodded and Tyler couldn't help but notice the sadness creeping into Emory's scrubbed features. Before he could censor himself, Tyler pointed out the sadness and added, "You don't feel sorry for him, do you?"

Emory evaded. "Did you come up here to snoop through my personal stuff?"

Tyler wanted to point out that he wasn't snooping. The bulletin board wasn't exactly hidden, was it? After all, it was in a prominent place, right there on the wall. But he didn't say any of those things. Instead, he reiterated that he simply wanted to see how Emory was doing. "I miss you."

Emory nodded. "Is that why, last time we were together, you sneaked out without so much as a goodbye?"

"I'm sorry about that, Em. I really am. I got a little spooked, I guess." He wanted it to seem he was spooked about commitment and not the fact that Emory was naked in a corner, mumbling to Jeffrey Dahmer, possibly after wetting the bed.

Again, what am I doing here?

You're holding out a hand to someone who might need it.

Emory nodded. He glanced at the bulletin board one time and then, taking Tyler's elbow, led him gently back toward the living room. "Why don't you sit down? Want a glass of water?"

"Water would be great." Tyler seated himself on the couch. "But if you have anything stronger, I'll drink to that." Tyler chuckled.

Emory shook his head. "I don't." He departed for the kitchen. Water ran. He returned in a moment with two glasses of water, a bit cloudy. Tyler took one and set it on the coffee table before him.

"So, are you working again?"

Emory shook his head. "No. Are you?"

Tyler told him again about his gig at the AMA. He was pretty sure he'd mentioned it to Emory when he ran into him at Sidetrack, but maybe he forgot. Emory listened, *again*, but it still was as though he didn't hear.

Silence grew, like a third presence, in the room.

At last, Emory veered off the small talk. "Why did you leave me?"

Tyler's mouth opened. He didn't know what to say. His first impulse was to deny, but he knew that wasn't true. He *had* left Emory, not only that morning months ago, after he let loose a bloodcurdling scream in bed next to him, but also in the months afterward, when he'd made no attempt to see him. He felt like a hypocrite sitting here now, in fact, confused and longing for the relief that he knew could be his if he'd only stand, cross the room, open the door, and head back out into the normal world.

He stayed put. And he realized Emory waited for an answer. There were times when Tyler knew it was best not to try to think of what he *should* say, but to simply speak from his heart.

"You scared me." There, it was out.

Emory didn't ask why. He simply sat back more fully on the couch, gaze straight ahead, waiting.

Tyler sucked in a breath and went on, telling Emory about the wet bed, the whispering in the corner of the room. "It was all just so strange. I didn't know how to handle it. I didn't know how to talk to you, what to say. So I bailed. I ran. I'm sorry." Tyler really didn't know how sorry he was. After all, his reaction was what he'd classify as human and self-protective.

After a while, Emory said, "I was just having a bad dream, that's all. And, for the record, I sweat a lot when I sleep. My body's like a furnace. I didn't pee the bed." He continued to stare ahead, not looking at Tyler. "You've probably said some weird things in your sleep too."

Tyler shrugged. "I wouldn't know. I'm never awake when I talk in my sleep."

"But someone might have heard you?"

"Always had my own room. And these days, when I might have a visitor or be visiting someone for a little slumber party, I always make an excuse to leave early." Tyler scooted over, closer to Emory. He touched his chin lightly, forcing Emory to look at him. "I'm sorry. You're right. I could have at least left you a note."

"You could have at least called me, or checked in on me, since you say you're concerned about me."

Tyler swallowed hard. Emory was right.

"You just didn't want to."

"No. No, I didn't." Tyler inched closer, so that their bodies were touching. "But I'm here now. And Emory? Never once did I forget you. I honestly doubt that a day went by that I didn't think of you. God knows why, but it's true."

He no longer needed to force Emory to look at him. He was staring intently at Tyler now, tears in his eyes. "Really? You mean that?"

"I wouldn't say it if I didn't mean it."

There was a long period of silence again. And Tyler wondered if he should go. The following day was Saturday and he had plans to meet up with Cole and the rest of the gang for brunch at a little diner near Rosehill Cemetery. That life, the one a few hours away, seemed as though it now belonged to some imaginary character, a guy in a movie or book, happy-go-lucky, without a care.

Tyler was taken by surprise as Emory leaned forward and gathered him up in his arms, squeezing Tyler so hard that Tyler could swear he felt the beat of Emory's heart. He was breathless, and he could tell Emory was too.

When they at last pulled away, there was no hesitation about looking deeply into the other's eyes. "So where does this leave us? You came by, you saw me, saw I was okay. At least that's what I think you see."

Tyler wasn't sure at all that was what he saw but nodded anyway. "You're good." He glanced down at the floor and then back up again. "Maybe we could start over? I don't know about the sex part or sleeping together, but just as friends? Take things slow? Have fun. For now?"

Emory smiled.

Tyler could see, in that smile, warmth and a real humanity. Maybe Tyler was wrong. Maybe there was nothing scarier here than a misguided soul, lonely and in need of being *seen*, just like Tyler's mother, once upon a time.

"Sure," Emory said at last. "Let's give it another shot."

And before Tyler could respond, Emory surprised him by getting up and crossing the room. He opened the door and stood there, hand on knob, waiting. "Next time you come by, make it at a decent hour, okay?"

Tyler laughed. "Okay."

He passed by Emory and could feel his gaze boring into him. He stopped near the door and groped in his pocket. He pulled out a plain white business card that had only his name and phone number on it. The cards had come in handy in the bars when he met someone he liked. "Keep this," he said. "And please, use it. I just got myself a brand-new answering machine."

Emory took the card and stuffed it into his own pocket. "Bye, Tyler."

Outside the building, a fog had fallen and it really was silent, no sound of traffic, or the L, everything was muffled.

Dead.

And Tyler, heading toward the train, wondered if he'd done the right thing or if he'd let his restless heart guide him in the wrong direction once more.

Chapter Fifteen

Emory hurried to the window to watch Tyler's silhouette get eaten up by the fog outside. Its gray tendrils rose from the sidewalk, consuming him until there was nothing left but his memory.

Emory shuddered at the touch of a hand on his shoulder, squeezing. He didn't dare turn, for fear there would be no one there. Instead, he froze, listening.

"You did the right thing," a man's voice said softly, close to his ear. "Letting him go like that. By doing that, you've already learned a lesson I never did—let them go. If they come back, then you really have something." The hand squeezed again, and Emory felt reassured, almost blissful. "I know he'll come back. And when he does, you can be ready to make sure he doesn't wander off into the fog again."

Emory stood for a long time, hoping the weight of this hand on his shoulder wouldn't vanish, as Tyler had into the fog. He watched as headlights, going north on Kenmore, pierced the gray mist. Continued to watch as various forms emerged—a man walking a Pit Bull, a couple of teenagers, maybe returning home from a rave, shoving each other, their laughter muffled, an old woman tugging a shopping cart behind her.

When at last he turned, he wasn't surprised.

There was no one there. Logically, he knew that—expected it. Yet the words spoken and the touch were as real as anything in his memory.

He moved to his bedroom, stripped out of his clothes, folded them neatly, and placed them in a neat stack on one of the ladderback chairs he'd appropriated from the dining room. He slid between the sheets and smiled.

Tyler came back.

He really came back.

He will come back again.

He was asleep, as was common for him these days, within minutes.

*

"Wake up, my little sleepy head!" Mother nudges me. My eyes flutter open to bright sunlight streaming into the room. The window's open. A warm summer breeze blows in.

Mother's leaving the room, quick, quick. Over her shoulder, she calls, "Breakfast's on the table, sweetie pie. Pancakes and sausages! I told Mary Helen to wait for you, but I doubt she did."

I rub my eyes and watch as Mother disappears around the corner.

Outside, someone honks relentlessly, and a man's voice calls, "Shut the fuck up! You're not sane. You never were!" Laughter.

The posters from my boyhood have been Scotch taped back up on the wall. There's Quentin, Barnabas, and Angelique from Dark Shadows. *How I loved that show! I'd run home from school every day to watch it. I wonder where Mother or Mary Helen found these old posters that I'd once so carefully put up. But then I look more closely around the room. It's my boyhood room— the maple twin bed, the old dresser with the top handle for the drawer missing, the baby blue walls. All of it changed back...*

I get up, noticing the striped shorty pajamas and how much smaller I am.

In the dining room, a little towheaded girl waits, hair in pigtails. A childhood Mary Helen. Her plate has a huge stack of pancakes on it, but instead of syrup, they're covered in blood. A little of the crimson alarm has dribbled onto the white linen place mat beneath.

She's arranged her sausages so that they resemble dismembered body parts.

My stomach does a somersault, and I turn to rush from the room, the bile splashing against the back of my throat.

I'm headed for the bathroom, but it's gone. A smooth wall is in the place of where the door once was.

And Mother and Mary Helen, somewhere behind me, their voices verging on hysteria, laugh and laugh at me.

*

Emory woke with a start, sitting bolt upright in bed, a just-dead scream still on his lips. The sheets were indeed wet and twisted around him, constricting him like a mummy. Muted light filtered in through his blinds. The roar of a garbage truck outside sounded like a monster.

Emory had to look around the room, with its walnut full bed and chest of drawers, its Van Gogh reproduction on the wall, the black-and-white TV on its little stand, to reassure himself he hadn't somehow returned to his boyhood room.

He trembled. Mary Helen and Mother had seemed so real. The whole dream was so authentic it made Emory ponder if this moment right now wasn't actually a dream. Was he really just a boy? Had his adult life and all that had happened to him been only a dream?

"Don't be ridiculous," he whispered. He tore the damp sheets off himself angrily, as though they were something with tentacles, holding him down. "You need to get a job. Get out of here. You'll be homeless soon."

He glanced at the little alarm clock on his nightstand. "Good Lord, it's after ten! You used to criticize Mary Helen for sleeping this late and here you are, following in her footsteps."

Emory forced himself up and out of bed and dressed quickly in the clothes he'd left out the night before. He hurried to the kitchen and started the coffee pot.

Waiting for the coffee to brew, he leaned against the Formica-topped counter and rubbed his eyes. Had Tyler really been here the night before? Or had that been a dream too?

Emory poured himself a cup of black coffee and took it with him into the living room. He sat on the couch for a while, trying to think where he could go to find a job today. Perhaps he could take the train out to one of the 'burbs that had a Home Depot and be one of the guys who lined the parking lot looking for work.

Except he was about as handy as his mother had been.

Maybe he could go downtown and put in applications at a few of the temporary agencies. That was how he'd found his job at Quality Investigations all those years ago.

He stared into his empty cup, grimacing at the black residue at the bottom. He felt uninspired and unmotivated as he had just about every day since Mother had died, since he'd decided not to return to work, since

Tyler had left him lying in piss-soaked sheets (yes, he knew).

He realized that, someday, necessity would force him to be part of the workforce once more. He also knew his options, with his limited experience and education, were limited. His most likely prospects would be in telemarketing or doing customer service from a call center. At least he wouldn't have to deal directly with people on a face-to-face basis.

But, he reasoned, one more day without job hunting wasn't going to cause his world to collapse, financial or otherwise. This month's rent was already paid. There was food in the fridge.

But Tyler? Now there was a subject that did induce something in him. It was so long since he'd felt anything akin to it, that it took a few minutes for Emory to recognize the sensation as pleasure, maybe even joy. Anticipation?

He visualized Tyler sitting close on the couch, only a few hours ago. How sweet that he'd come by to check on him, even if it had been a very long time since he'd visited. Emory made excuses for Tyler—he was young, he was confused, he wanted to play the field before he realized what he had with Emory—but in the end, he believed Tyler when he claimed that he'd thought of Emory nearly every day, even though he wasn't seeing him on a regular basis.

Tyler's sweet face, his piercing eyes and gaze, and the warmth of his body next to Emory's motivated him. He sprang from the couch with renewed energy and went into the kitchen, where he washed out his cup and set it in the dish drainer to dry.

He was showered and dressed within fifteen minutes and out the door in twenty.

Outside, the fog had burned off to reveal a brilliant day, filled with sunshine and a nearly cloudless blue sky. Only a few strands of cloud hovered in strips above Lake Michigan.

And, for the first time in the longest time, Emory felt he had purpose.

There was an Ace Hardware store on Broadway within walking distance.

He headed briskly south on Broadway, enjoying the sun on his face, the undercurrent of warmth in the breeze. He didn't even mind his fellow pedestrians nor the traffic going by on this busy thoroughfare. For once, Emory felt he was part of humanity.

He passed a Dominick's grocery store and paused. A light bulb clicked on over his head. "I'll make him a nice dinner. That's what I'll do." Wasn't Mother always saying that the way to a man's heart was through his stomach? He veered off his course, navigated through the parking lot and the front doors of the grocery store.

Inside, as usual, it was much too cold. Even with his eyes adjusted to the sunlight outside, the fluorescents in the store seemed too bright, making Emory blink. Even the Muzak playing over the store's PA system seemed off, surreal. It was an instrumental version of Michael Jackson's song, "Beat It."

Emory immediately recalled the Weird Al Yankovic parody of the song, "Eat It" and remembered how he and Mary Helen laughed and laughed when they played it on the radio. Thinking of Mary Helen's laughter made him recall his dream from that morning—and the bloody pancakes.

He almost turned around and headed back outside.

But he told himself he was being ridiculous. "It was just a dream, after all. It didn't mean anything." He didn't realize he was speaking aloud until he noticed a woman near the display of citrus fruits, eyeing him over pince-nez glasses.

"What are you looking at?" he asked her.

She didn't respond with a verbal answer. She lowered her head as she sorted through lemons and limes.

What should I make for him? Emory made sure to keep his thoughts internal.

The Muzak answered for him. As though reading his mind, it shifted from "Beat It" to "Cheeseburger in Paradise." Emory headed for the meat section.

Laden with a couple plastic bags of ground chuck, American cheese slices, buns, a ready-made coleslaw, and a six-pack of Old Style, Emory continued south to Ace Hardware.

There, he'd get the other things on his mental shopping list—a length of strong rope, duct tape, and chloroform if they had it.

Whistling, he continued on his way.

Once home, he put away his purchases and then sat in the living room to call Tyler.

"This is Tyler Kay. Leave a message at the sound of the beep."

Emory paused and took a deep breath. "Hello Tyler. It's Emory Hughes. I was wondering if you'd like to come over for dinner. Maybe tonight even? Or sometime soon? Please return this call and let me know when you're available." He almost said, "Or if you're even interested," but then thought he'd sound pathetic.

He hung up.

At last—hope.

sniffed. There was one of Kung Pao shrimp, another of Mongolian beef, and a third of white rice. All three smelled slightly off. It was no wonder. He'd ordered this food when Cole was over almost two weeks ago. He jettisoned them into the trash.

He peered again into the chilled and very empty fridge. He opened the few cupboards he had and was confronted with Cheerios, a bag of sugar, two cans of kidney beans, and a package of angel hair pasta.

Dispirited, he sat back down in the living room area and wondered about ordering in a pizza.

The phone rang.

"Tyler?" Emory's nervousness was apparent in his soft voice.

"Hey buddy. How you doin'?"

"I'm all right, thank you." He went silent for a few moments, and Tyler was about to say something, *anything*, to break the silence when Emory said, "I was wondering if you got my message."

"Yeah, yeah, I just listened to it. It was a nice surprise...and I'd love to come over for dinner. That's sweet of you."

Emory cut him off. "Tonight?"

Tyler looked at the clock on his VCR. It was already going on eight o'clock. "Oh, I don't know, man. I'm beat. I had a hell of a long day."

Silence rose as a response. Tyler swore he could almost feel disappointment making its way through the phone lines. At last Emory said, "Okay."

"But another time? Rain check?"

"Sure. Of course." Another pause. "Well, I should be going." But he didn't go. He stayed on the line, not saying anything.

Even though everything in Tyler was telling him to stay home tonight, even if it meant eating plain pasta with Cheerios for dinner, he said, "Isn't it awfully late?"

"Not for me," Emory answered. "And I have stuff all ready to go. Burgers, coleslaw, even some French fries."

Mention of the food made Tyler's stomach growl and prompted him to ask, "Is there anything I can bring?"

"Just yourself," Emory said, cheerful at last.

*

When Tyler got off the train, he paused in front of the Forge. The door swung open as a couple of patrons emerged into the neon-lit darkness of Granville Avenue. The bar was fairly crowded for a weeknight, the revelers lit up by electric blue and red signs advertising Old Style and Bud and the TV over the bar, which was showing some ancient porn—*Boys in the Sand*, maybe. There was a lot of deep male laughter, conversation, and the clinking of glasses.

The Forge looked very inviting.

He stood on the sidewalk for a moment, contemplating whether he should slip in and have a quick gin and tonic to take the edge off his fatigue and, yes, dread, at the evening ahead. He knew Emory was unlikely to have any hard liquor to offer up, so the idea of a drink was tempting.

But in the end, he pictured Emory sitting alone in his apartment. That thought made Tyler flash on a scene from an old black-and-white movie he'd seen when he'd been far too young to understand it. *The Last Picture Show.* The scene that came up on the interior screen of his mind was with Cloris Leachman, as the small-town Texas wife of the local high school football coach, waiting in vain for her teenage lover to show up. She was in a darkened room sitting on the bed in a white dress. The stark, shadowed image cried out loneliness and despair. He remembered how sad this simple moment was, because the audience knew the boy would never show up. And he was the only light in her love- and attention-starved life.

Go! Go! He's waiting for you.

Tyler continued to Emory's high-rise apartment building.

He relaxed some when Emory opened the door to him. In a pair of sweats and a red Bulls T-shirt, he appeared less crazed than he had the night Tyler ran into him at Sidetrack. In fact, he looked kind of delicious, a little thuggish, a skinhead fantasy. Tyler grinned. The fatigue vanished as he stepped around Emory and into his apartment.

He sniffed. "Something smells good."

Emory said, "I've got hamburgers on the stove, sizzling away in Mother's old cast-iron skillet. I'm cooking them in butter and Worcestershire sauce, just like she did. She called them sizzle burgers and we just loved 'em." He eyed Tyler. "I hope you will too."

Tyler proceeded to the couch and sat.

"Let me make sure our burgers don't burn! Medium rare, right?"

Tyler nodded.

"I'll grab you a beer while I'm in the kitchen, okay?"

Tyler realized how parched he was; the beer sounded like a gift.

When Emory came back holding two cans of beer, he was smiling. "I turned off the heat on the burgers. They were pretty rare, but they're tented under foil, so they'll continue to cook. I've also got coleslaw and some tater tots."

"Oh my God, I love tater tots."

Emory nodded. "Me too. And there's an apple pie for dessert."

"Did you make it?"

"Nah. I couldn't ever compete with Mother's apple pie. Hers was simply the best in the world, no exaggeration. She used walnuts, raisins, and a touch of maple in hers, but I don't know what the ratios of each were. I didn't even try. It's just good old Dominick's bakery. Hope that's okay."

"I'm sure it's all going to be really good."

"I hope you're right." Emory glanced at the unopened can of beer in Tyler's hand. "Oh! Where are my manners? You need a glass!"

Tyler popped open the can. "No need."

"No, no! What kind of host would I be if let you drink out of a *can*? Besides, beer is better when poured into a glass to release its bouquet."

Tyler handed the can of Old Style back. "If you say so. I'm hardly a connoisseur."

Emory stood. "Me either. But I was raised right. Gimme." He gestured for Tyler to hand him the can.

Emory disappeared into the kitchen. Tyler stood and stooped in front of an ancient hi-fi, a relic from the 1960s, he imagined. Next to it was a stack of record albums— Andy Williams, Jerry Vale, The Boston Pops. The most recent one was a collection of The Mamas and the Papas greatest hits. *Doesn't this guy listen to any music ever? These must have been his mom's!* Tyler shrugged and took The Mamas and the Papas collection out of its sleeve. He placed it on the turntable and watched it drop into place, the arm with the needle sliding over and lowering itself onto the spinning disc.

"California Dreamin'" began playing.

Emory hurried into the room, frowning. He glanced at the record player and then at Tyler. "That belongs to Mother."

"Is it okay? I thought it would be nice to have a little music with dinner."

Emory looked at him as though he'd suggested bringing in belly dancers and a team of performing elephants to accompany their burgers and tots. But then he shrugged and said, "Sure. Nice."

He returned to the kitchen and came back holding aloft two mugs of beer, heavy with foam heads. "Here you go!" He set Tyler's on the coffee table in front of him, beneath a paper towel.

Tyler leaned forward and lifted his glass. "To renewing our friendship."

The toast pleased Emory, who smiled. He clinked his glass against Tyler's. "Amen to that. And maybe more than friendship?"

Tyler cocked his head. "Okay. We'll see."

"Yes, we shall." Emory drained half of his beer in one long gulp. He then peered at the beer in Tyler's hand. "Drink up. You don't want it to get warm."

"Oh, it won't be around long enough for *that*." Tyler laughed and took a big drink. The beer tasted good, cold and bracing. But after it had gone down, Tyler licked his lips and couldn't resist making a little face.

"Everything okay?" Emory eyed him, leaning in closer.

"Sure, it's fine." He paused. "Did you have a chalky aftertaste from your beer?"

Emory shook his head and allowed himself another long swallow. "Tastes fine to me." He belched and then giggled. "Drink up. Supper's almost ready."

But Emory didn't get up. He watched and waited for Tyler to drink more of his beer. "Down the hatch," he urged, and Tyler was reminded of fraternity parties from when he was in college, when the object of drinking beer was to chug as much of the stuff as fast as possible—you know, to prove how manly one was.

The aftertaste remained, but Tyler finished the beer anyway. Emory seemed to expect it. When the glass was empty, Emory grabbed it and stood. "Refills! And I'll get supper on the table. Gimme a couple minutes."

Tyler watched Emory leave the room. He was glad he'd come over and hadn't given in to his fatigue. The guy was a strange one, that much was for sure, but there was something in him that resonated with Tyler, that made him want to, if not fix, then be there for him.

He laid his head back on the couch and closed his eyes as he listened to The Mamas and the Papas sing "Do you Wanna Dance?" Tyler had always thought the song was a Bette Midler original and was surprised to hear this version. Still, it was a gorgeous rendition of a romantic song, and it relaxed him further. He smiled, rather than feared, how heavy his limbs suddenly felt, as though weighted down, and at the burning sensation just behind his eyelids. It *had* been a long day. He sank back into the cushions of the couch, feeling oddly at home. Beneath the music was the sound of water running in the kitchen, meat sizzling, cupboards opening and closing, and the slap of the refrigerator door shutting.

For a reason he couldn't fathom, the moment reminded him of being in bed as a child, safe and secure, and listening to the sound of the television downstairs and his parents' occasional laughter and conversation. He felt safe. And safer still when they would, together, mount the stairs and come to bed themselves. When they were all tucked in for the night, their big house dark, he could relax and sleep.

Tyler wondered what Emory would make of him if he asked, "Do you wanna dance?"

*

They stand, almost in a formal pose, holding each other close. Music, lush, swells up. An orchestra. And Emory begins to glide Tyler around the room. But where are they? The light is diffuse. Shadows lurk in the corners. There are no windows, only plain white walls that rise up and up until they disappear into these same queer shadows.

Mist swirls around them as they spin.

Tyler places his head on Emory's shoulder and closes his eyes, transported, wrapped in heat and security.

*

Tyler woke to a hammer banging. *Is that bang, bang, bang what's making my head throb with pain?* He turned and his head pounded and ached even more. He worried that he was about to throw up.

The worry became real, a self-fulfilling prophecy. He lifted his head a couple of inches off the hardwood and up came a yellow bile, acidic, choking him. It splashed onto the floor beneath him and Tyler could do nothing more than stare at the puddle as though it were something foreign rather than something that had emerged from his own body.

And at last, he opened his eyes, just a crack.

His vision blurred, then focused. Pale light verged on darkness, but not so dim that he couldn't see Emory, wearing only a pair of white Fruit-of-the-Loom briefs, standing at what appeared to be a small window. He was nailing boards over the glass. The light filtering in through the cracks in the wood appeared orange as though it might be coming from a streetlamp outside.

Tyler wiped his mouth and even though it made his stomach roil anew, got up on his elbows and tried to squeak out a few words, which sounded very much to his buzzing ears like, "What the fuck?"

Emory continued to hammer the last board in place.

"What the fuck?" Tyler repeated, louder this time. Panic was rising in him like a flight of bumblebees taking wing and swarming inside his body.

Slowly, Emory turned and peered down. He smiled kindly.

This isn't right.

Panic rose, making Tyler's heart pound so rapidly and with such force he feared it might burst through his chest. He barely held the nausea in check. Sweat slid from his hairline into his eyes; it trickled down his spine. He tried to swallow, but there was no spit in his mouth. His tongue felt like sandpaper.

This isn't right.

This isn't right.

A monstrous sense of terror rose. Tyler turned and tried to get to his knees as step one to rising to his feet. But when he attempted this, he collapsed back to the floor, dizzy and panting.

My feet are bound.

His ankles were close together, the bones scraping against each other, sheathed in wrap after wrap of duct tape.

"Emory? Emory, what's going on? What are you *doing*, man?"

Emory had a hammer in one hand, and it made Tyler cringe. He was grateful as Emory set it on the floor. He squatted beside Tyler, who now realized at some point Emory had removed all of Tyler's own clothing.

Emory swiped Tyler's forehead with the palm of his hand, wiping away the slick sheen of sweat. He put his hand to his mouth and licked. "Salty," he pronounced. "Shh, shh now. Don't you worry that pretty little head. Old Emory here, for once in his life, has everything under control."

Quickly, Emory grabbed a roll of duct tape Tyler hadn't noticed from the floor and even more quickly, wrapped a length of it around Tyler's wrists, binding them together.

"Why? Why are you doing this? Emory! I thought we were friends."

Emory's face drew near, and Tyler shut his eyes and held his breath at the smell of meat issuing from Emory's mouth when he spoke. "It's all gonna be okay. This is for your own good. For *our* good. You'll see."

"What are you talking about?" Tyler tried to wriggle his hands free, but it only upped the pain and nausea plaguing him. He scooted back a little on his ass, away from Emory. He had enough sense now to look around him.

They were in a walk-in closet. Dresses hung from hangers, some flowery prints, others made of heavier fabric, in various shades of royal blue, purple, and a deep crimson. Brocade? Hat boxes lined one shelf. Above that, a couple of suitcases and a stack of sweaters. "How is this for my own good? Where are we?"

Emory moved close again and poked Tyler playfully in the chest. "We're in my apartment, silly. You knew that. More specifically, we're in Mother's closet. I'm going to drag a mattress and some bedding in here for you if you behave. And I can tell you can use a glass of water." He touched Tyler's lips. "They're all dry. Yuck."

No words came to Tyler's muddled mind. His mouth hung open, and he could do nothing more than simply stare.

This wasn't happening. Not really. It couldn't be. The dream he was having earlier? The one about slow dancing with Emory? What was happening here and now was simply the result of that very pleasant dream betraying him and morphing into nightmare.

As much as Tyler tried to convince himself that where he was *right now* and what was occurring in this cramped and claustrophobic closet smelling sickeningly of mothballs, he couldn't deny how the hardwood floor made his tailbone and spine ache, how his stomach roiled like the waves on Lake Michigan. The physical pain and the sickness were rude and crude reminders that this was no dream.

Emory is keeping me prisoner?

Laughter burbled up inside, spilled out over his parched lips. Again, he tried to tell himself this wasn't really happening. The alternative was to believe what was right before his eyes and that was simply unacceptable. Being poisoned (the fact of that just dawned on him—horrifyingly) and bound in a closet? That shit happened in novels, something by Dean Koontz, Stephen King, or maybe Jack Ketchum. Tyler's life revolved around a stupid, dead-end job that he was too good for, getting drunk on the weekends and having sex with strangers. It was what twentysomething gay boys did in the 1990s.

"This isn't really happening."

Tyler thought he'd said the words only in his head, to himself. But Emory stiffened a bit at the words, cocking his head. "Silly. Of course, this is really happening. This is the beginning of our new life together."

"You're nuts." Rage gradually started to eclipse Tyler's terror. "You can't do this." His breath quickened and he told himself, internally this time, to calm the fuck down. *Getting even crazier than he is right now will do you no good.* "Emory? This isn't necessary, man. Unwrap this tape, okay? We can literally come out of the closet and talk about this. Talk about what you need and how I can help."

"How you can help? You think I need help?" Emory giggled. "The only one that needs help right now is you, mister." He stood quickly and Tyler could see, to his disgust and queasiness, an erection poking out the front of Emory's tighty-whities. There was also a piss stain along the front. *God save me.*

Emory stared down at him, helpless on the floor. "I'll be back in a bit."

And almost before Tyler knew what was happening, Emory was gone.

Tyler tried to swallow again as Emory slid a deadbolt into place—on the outside of the closet door. He lay back down and curled up on his side, drawing his knees up to his chest. Groggy and exhausted, he closed his eyes and prayed for the oblivion of sleep. Maybe when he reawakened, he'd be in a better place to fight—or use his wits to get out of this mess.

You should have known better.

Chapter Seventeen

Cole Hardwick was sad.

Sometimes, it seemed everything about his life was as sad as the dinner he was putting together at this very moment—a microwaved frozen entrée, which consisted of a dry chicken breast with a salty yellow sauce, fake mashed potatoes, and a pile of wrinkled peas and carrots. His apartment here in the Rogers Park neighborhood of Chicago was sad. Even though the area bordered Lake Michigan, Cole's apartment was set far back from its shores, a good mile west, on a busy area of Touhy Avenue. The traffic noise ceased only for a short time in the wee small hours of the morning. The place was only about six-hundred square feet and came furnished with threadbare stuff that he could have improved on at any thrift store in the city. His neighbor below seemed to love nothing more than fighting with his boyfriend, smoking cigarettes, and cooking cabbage, all of which Cole bore witness to on a daily basis.

Sad. His TV was on the fritz, so he had the radio on, tuned to alternative rock station WXRT. The DJ talking was a cruel reminder of how alone he was. This was what passed for company in his world.

The couch groaned in protest as he lowered himself on it. He set his bottle of Bud Lite on the coffee table before him, along with his microwaved dinner, which he'd attempted to make more homey by putting on one of his dinner plates. Sad.

He sighed, took a swig of beer, and dug in. Someday, he needed to learn to cook. Maybe tomorrow? He could crack open that classic his parents had given him when he'd graduated from Northern Illinois University Chicago Circle, *The Joy of Cooking*. He'd been meaning to start trying some of its recipes for ten years now and never once had actually acted upon the plan. It was always easy to order a pizza or just nuke something as he'd done tonight.

What he was *really* sad about, though, was one Mr. Tyler Kay. He was supposed to have met Cole for lunch today downtown at the Walnut Room, the signature restaurant of the flagship Marshall Fields where Cole had begun working only today. Cole had been primed for a festive, if not romantic, occasion.

They were going to celebrate his new job and finding employment after what seemed an endless time—six months of searching.

"Hey buddy, I'm gonna treat you to lunch on your first day," Tyler had said a few days ago over beers at Little Jim's. "And I'm sparing no expense. We're going to the Walnut Room, so all your coworkers can see us together and get jealous." He'd laughed and winked at Cole. Cole thought Tyler had been reading his mind. It had been a gloriously happy moment for Cole, who took Tyler's invitation as a date, whether that had been Tyler's intent or not.

He'd looked forward to their meet-up all morning and the anticipatory high energized him, made him even more cheerful than his usual outgoing self. He'd sold three suits that morning, and his manager had been impressed. He told him it was rare to have such awesome beginner's luck.

He got away a few minutes early for lunch and headed to the Walnut Room, hoping Tyler would already be there. He pictured him in a clean, white button-down and gray slacks, his blond hair gelled neatly into place, pale-blue eyes shimmering. He'd be waiting at the table and would have a card and a small gift as a token of good luck for Cole's first day.

Maybe he was letting his imagination run away with him. But still, he'd been thrilled Tyler had actually initiated them getting together for once. Cole had had a crush on the guy for months now and had spent many hours locked in Tyler's embrace—in dreams and fantasies that Cole prayed would one day become real. This lunch, maybe, was a step toward that dream being fulfilled.

He'd unfolded his napkin, still riding a high from his successful morning, and ordered a bowl of French onion soup while he waited.

And waited.

He'd finished the soup and it was only when he had ten minutes remaining in his lunch hour that he realized Tyler wouldn't be showing up. The soup's pungent flavor now tasted acidic, sour in the back of his throat. The bright, sunny day outside only served to make him feel more depressed, deflated, and defeated. Like a loser...

He'd grudgingly accepted Tyler may never return his feelings. But he didn't expect the guy would stand him up! At the very least, Cole'd assumed they were good friends. Even friends didn't make a lunch date and then just not bother appearing without so much as a word of explanation.

When there was only a minute or two left, Cole paid for his soup and went back to work. He tried to put on a smiling mask, but his heart was no longer in the job. He'd sold only a tie and a trio of black socks that afternoon, and he attributed his lack of success to the fact that he was most likely radiating failure. Thank God he'd had such a good morning.

And now he sat alone and lonely in his cramped, characterless, and cheerless apartment, forcing down food he wasn't enjoying and wondering about Tyler. He'd called his number at work and had been told he hadn't come in that day. He'd called his home and left several messages for him.

No word. Nothing. And the rejection really hurt. To Cole, it seemed this was standard operating procedure for young gay men these days—to simply not call and to vanish, even if you thought you'd made a connection. It had happened to Cole one too many times for his liking. No, make that a hundred too many times. A friend had once told him he was "too nice for his own good." Cole shrugged. He'd never understood how that was even possible.

He never, though, expected Tyler to treat him this way—to just vanish. They shared, he believed, at least something that could last as a friendship, even if would sadly go no further.

The evening, long, dark, and uneventful, stretched out before him. No TV and he'd returned that Stephen King book, *Needful Things* to the library last week. He could shower and head out to a bar, but he didn't feel inspired to be around crowds. He was also reluctant and pessimistic. He'd just stand against the wall, a beer clenched in his fist, and be ignored. Standard operating procedure.

He wanted to be around Tyler. No other man, no matter what he looked like, could compare. Cole wished it wasn't so, but the heart wanted what it wanted.

And if Tyler wasn't showing up and wasn't answering his phone, maybe there was something wrong. It didn't have to necessarily mean Tyler was avoiding him. To think so was evidence that his self-esteem needed a good kick in the ass. He wasn't necessarily being blown off. Tyler could be sick or in trouble. He might need Cole's help.

Or he could just be avoiding you. His mind could be relentless—his worst enemy.

Or he could be holed up with some hottie he met at Sidetrack. Case in point.

Cole shook his head, imagining slapping himself in the face, and forced himself to get up off the couch. He needed to do *something*.

*

Cole got off the L at Western and walked the two or three blocks to Tyler's new digs on Lincoln Avenue. The street was still alive with hustle and bustle, even though it was getting late. People window-shopping in Lincoln Square, catching a movie at the Davis, or hanging out in one of the many cafés, restaurants, and bars. All of this made Cole feel paradoxically hopeful and depressed because his aloneness set him apart from everyone he passed. Even folks walking alone at least had a dog for company.

He rang Tyler's intercom button several times. He stepped back to look up at the window he knew faced the street and noted there were no lights on. *This is a fool's errand. He's not home. And you should be. You need to get a good night's sleep and be bright-eyed and bushy-tailed for the sales floor tomorrow.* He rang once more. No answer.

He turned back to the street, thinking about getting a cup of coffee or maybe a doughnut, which he knew he didn't need, but at least the sweet would give him a little comfort.

It began to drizzle, and Cole noted how the precipitation matched his mood.

There was a Dunkin' Donuts over on Western, so Cole headed over there. A buttermilk glazed and a large coffee with three sugars and lots of half-and-half would be just the thing to turn around his foul mood. Or, at least in theory... He knew once he'd consumed all those calories and considered his ever-expanding girth, he'd feel differently.

Still, maybe this time, he'd be lucky, and the treats would do the trick, turning a depressing night into a happy one. *Buddy, it never works.*

After he'd ordered at the counter, he sat at one of the booths in the too-bright restaurant, feeling conspicuous, as though the other patrons were judging him and thinking, *right. That's the last thing he needs.*

Sometimes, Cole was his own worst enemy.

As he was finishing his coffee, the two buttermilk sinkers now literally a crummy memory, he had a strange thought, one that had the potential to galvanize. He didn't know where it came from. He certainly never considered himself any kind of psychic, and he would say his intuition was, at best, faulty and unreliable, but a thought appeared in his head, clear as could be, as though there were someone outside himself talking to him.

Help me.

The words flashed in his mind in red neon. And he heard Tyler saying them.

Cole stared out at the darkness pressing against the plate glass windows and shivered.

"I'd like to," he whispered to himself. "But where do I start?"

He went out into the rain and decided on a course of action. He'd call Tyler's work in the morning, see if they had any idea where he might be. He clung to the hope that there was a good explanation for his silence, other than he was bored with Cole, or he'd found himself a boyfriend who was consuming all his time and energy.

If that didn't work, he'd track down Tyler's family.

This just didn't feel right.

Help me.

Chapter Eighteen

Tyler was asleep.

That made Emory feel good, as though it was evidence of how comfortable Tyler had become here, as a guest in his house. He stood, framed in the doorway to Mother's closet, looking down on Tyler's sleeping form, the way he was curled up on one side, his knees drawn up to his chest, snoring. Emory's lips turned up in a little smile. He regarded the bowl of oatmeal with its brown sugar, raisins, and cream that he'd brought for Tyler. It could be a perfect morning if only Tyler would cooperate and see how well-meaning this all was.

I'm not really keeping him prisoner. I'm just training him, like one would do with a dog. I want him to know he's safe and secure. And I need this time of confinement simply to show him how it all works. I know the day will arrive when I can loosen up what binds him, let him out of this closet, and he'll exist with me, side-by-side, my soul mate. We'll be a real couple, happy at last.

He squatted to set the bowl on the floor. The clunk on the floor roused Tyler, whose eyelids fluttered open. He regarded Emory with a mystified stare.

Emory laughed. "You look like you're seeing a ghost! Or maybe you forgot who I am." He tussled Tyler's hair, which was greasy to the touch. He jerked his hand away when Tyler recoiled, pulling back.

"You'll learn," Emory whispered. He paused for a moment and then pointed at the bowl of oatmeal, above which rose wisps of steam. "You must be hungry. I made you Mother's famous steel-cut oats. You have to cook them for a half hour. No minute oats for you, young man. And I added a lot of brown sugar, so it's super yummy."

He didn't want to interpret the look on Tyler's face as a glare, so he simply tried to make himself believe his expression was one of interest, maybe even hunger.

"Why are you doing this?" Tyler's voice came out as a croak, which made Emory realize how long he'd gone without water. He stood and hurried from the closet to grab him a glass of water from the tap in the bathroom, the closest source.

When he returned, Tyler had scooted out of the closet. The morning light hit his naked body and Emory grimaced. He'd soiled himself during the night, and the visual and olfactory evidence of that was a turnoff. "We need to get you in the bath." He squatted down and held the glass up to Tyler's lips, who turned his head away.

"Tsk! Now, don't be like that, Ty. I know you're thirsty."

Patiently, Emory waited beside him on the floor. Finally, after only a few seconds, Emory got his reward when Tyler turned his head back and took a few sips. "Good boy," Emory whispered. "Now, you need to scoot yourself back into the closet. I brought in the mattress for you and the covers." He frowned. "Although I need to get most of that stuff down to the basement now and get them washed." Emory realized he'd been a little rash in this decision and hadn't considered all the possibilities, distasteful, that might arise when keeping a human guest.

After Tyler had swallowed a little more than half the glass of water, Emory asked, "Are you ready for that oatmeal now? We don't want it to get cold."

"How am I supposed to eat it?" Tyler held up his hands, clasped together as though in prayer and bound at the wrist with duct tape. Emory thought he could feed him, like a baby. *But that's no way to treat a grown man.*

Emory cocked his head. "Tyler, you know I'm just doing this so we can be together."

"By force?"

"Don't look at it like that. I'm working on the advice of a friend."

"Dahmer?"

Emory smiled. "How did you know?"

"I've seen all the clippings. Since I first met you, I've noticed how fascinated you are by him." Tyler's gaze cut away from Emory as though he was afraid to regard him. "You feel like, what, you share some affinity with him or something?"

"I do. We do share an affinity." Emory slid the oatmeal aside and lay next to Tyler even though he smelled. "We've been writing to each other since he first got arrested."

Tyler stared at him, his mouth twitching. "He writes to you? From prison? They allow that?"

Emory nodded. He felt proud. "We're regular pen pals, Tyler. I may be the only person on the planet who understands him."

"You *understand* a serial killer? A cannibal?" Tyler rolled away from Emory, presenting his back. Emory tried to ignore the smear of shit on his backside and the smell that went with it, but the odor was so strong and repellent, it was hard to do.

Emory placed a hand on Tyler's shoulder and rolled him back, so he could look him in the eye. "Tyler," he whined. "It's not like that. He's just like you and me. He wants love. He never *wanted* to hurt anybody. That's the truth." Emory leaned close to Tyler's ear. "Just like I don't want to hurt you. I want you to know how much I care about you."

Tyler's eyes welled with tears, and Emory couldn't understand. "Why are you sad? I just want you to stay."

"Well, I guess Dahmer would get that," Tyler spat.

"Don't be that way." Emory stood. "Would you like to hear one of his letters?"

Tyler said nothing, so Emory took his silence as a yes and hurried to his desk to find the latest missive from Jeff.

He returned with the letter, which was in his mailbox only this morning. The mailman must have forgotten to deliver it yesterday because it was all alone. And the mail usually didn't arrive until midafternoon.

He held it to his side and gawked down at Tyler, who'd curled himself up in a little ball on Mother's bedroom floor and was sobbing. "Oh no," Emory whispered, kneeling beside him. The smell of feces rose. Emory leaned back and away on his haunches, in danger of tipping over backward.

He set the letter on the floor. "Stay here," he said and realized how pointless it was. "And don't make any noise. I don't want to have to gag you. I want us to talk this out." Before Tyler could reply, Emory hurried off to the bathroom, where he wet a couple washcloths with warm water. He rubbed a little soap on each. He started out and then returned to grab a stick of deodorant from the medicine cabinet.

When he returned, Tyler lay silently on the floor. Limp, he simply let Emory clean him up. When Emory was through and had succeeded in helping Tyler scoot over to the couch in the living room where he leaned against it, still on the floor, Emory gathered up the soiled bedding in a big ball, readying it for the laundry room. He sighed and went about making up a clean bed in the closet. "You're going to be a lot of work," he said to no one.

Finally, he came back with the oatmeal and a spoon. "I'm sorry. This is cold now. But please eat. It'll still fill you up."

Tyler stared, saying nothing. When Emory brought the first spoonful of cereal up, Tyler opened his mouth. Emory was pleased that he ate the entire bowl of oats and finished his water.

He retrieved the letter and came to sit beside Tyler, their backs against the couch, the morning sunlight slanting in through the blinds. The scene felt cozy, and Emory leaned into the hominess of it. He wasn't used to this.

"This was what he wrote, just this morning. I told him all about you." Emory smiled broadly at Tyler, but Tyler seemed to look right through him.

*

Dear Emory,

Tyler sounds like a keeper. Love is hard to find in this world, but when we do find it, we have to do whatever it takes to hold on. It doesn't always work. I'm living proof of that. No matter how hard I tried, I could never get someone to simply be by my side, to take this journey we call life together.

I never thought it was too much to ask.

I never believed I was hurting anyone. Well, at least until after it was too late. And I felt horrible! Emory, I really did. But there was something inside me—a little bit of hell that ate me up, that wouldn't let go, even when I knew I was crossing the most dangerous and wicked lines.

But back to Tyler. Take your time with him. Show him you care. If he doesn't see this, make him see it. If your love for him is a pure thing, and I know it is, he'll eventually see that and want to return it to you, maybe even tenfold.

I wish you luck with this young man, my friend. Don't worry about who you are. Don't worry about what you are. Cling to the belief that love is possible.

It's all we have in this world, really.

And Emory, I am so glad you're there for me.

I'm rooting for you, from all the way behind these prison walls.

Love,

Jeff

*

Emory set the letter on the floor and glanced over at Tyler to gauge his reaction. He thought it was a beautiful letter, charming in its own way. It stirred Emory's heart. It proved that Jeffrey Dahmer, despite the horror of his crimes, wasn't the monster the media made him out to be. He was simply a man caught up in dreadful circumstances, needing something desperately, but life hadn't given him the clues regarding how to get it.

He thought Tyler might see the same.

After a time, Emory spoke, "Well? What did you think?"

Slowly, Tyler turned to him. "About the letter?"

"Of course about the letter!" Emory hadn't meant to snap. But it was so obvious. What else would he have been talking about? His mother's oatmeal?

"Do you *really* think he wrote that to you?" Tyler eyed him with what looked like wariness, suspicion.

And that question gave Emory pause. What an odd thing to say! "Who else would have written it?" Emory bit his lip hard, wishing he could call back the anger and upset in his voice.

Tyler smiled, but the smile was as enigmatic as the Mona Lisa's. "Come on, Emory."

"I don't know what you're talking about." Emory rose from the floor, feeling a little shaken, a little sick to his stomach. A weird chill and a flutter of dizziness passed through him, and he sat down quickly on the couch for a moment to compose himself. He turned his head to look out the window. The sun had come up full, shining brightly. The sky was a brilliant shade of blue, unobscured by even one cloud. The world outside was coming alive. It was real.

He got up and moved to the kitchen where he'd left the duct tape. He came back to the living room, and when Tyler spied what he had in his hand, he flinched. "Emory. No. You don't need to. I promise—I'll be quiet."

Emory knelt and quickly bit off a piece of the tape.

"No."

But Emory slapped the tape across Tyler's lips, patting it into place along his stubbled cheeks. Tyler began to whimper beneath the silver tape.

But Emory was unaffected. He moved to Tyler's feet and roughly grabbed his ankles and dragged him across the living room floor, across his mother's bedroom, and back into her walk-in closet. He wrestled Tyler onto the mattress and stood, out of breath.

"I need to get your bedding washed up. And then you'll be all warm and comfy."

He turned and wished he could close his ears to the pleading, crying, and screaming trying to emerge from beneath the duct tape. The noise both angered and hurt him. He was only trying to help.

He quickly closed the door and locked it behind him. The sounds Tyler made weren't quite gone, but they were muffled.

Emory went into the living room, where The Mamas and the Papas *Greatest Hits* album was still on the old turntable. He switched it on and turned up the volume loud as "California Dreamin'" came on. If Tyler were to begin banging or kicking, Emory hoped the music would drown him out. He didn't know his neighbors, never had any interest. And now would not be the time to start.

He sat, listening for a moment. It had gone quiet in the closet. Then he leaned over, picked up the letter still on the floor with a trembling hand and stared at it.

After a while, he rose and placed it with the other letters on his desk.

He gathered up the soiled bedding and headed out to the laundry room.

Chapter Nineteen

Mary Helen paced outside the redbrick high-rise on Kenmore Avenue that she'd once called home. She wished she still smoked, but Liz had convinced her to give up the habit about a month ago. Nonetheless, she longed for the way a cigarette would calm her nerves, make the conversation she was about to have a little easier to broach. *Help me delay the inevitable...*

She sighed, gazing out at her old street. Cars ranging from rusting heaps to Mercedes Benzes and BMWs crowded the curbs. The strip of brown grass that ran along the edge of the sidewalk was littered with old cans and food wrappers. At the north end of the street, a Loyola University building stood, looking imposing. She felt as though she were standing in a canyon, the tall buildings drowning her in their sun-blocking shadows.

The damp air had a faint fishy tang.

Heavy storm clouds, gray, marched slowly across the sky. They reminded her she wouldn't be able to linger out here too long before the deluge the weather reports were predicting began. The chill in the air seeped into her bones.

But Lord, she didn't want to go inside even if it was warm. She didn't look forward to confronting her older brother to see what could be done.

But she had to. He was family.

She still ached with remorse for how she'd avoided her mother during her last days, rationalizing her guilt by claiming it was simply too painful to spend time with a woman who was being eaten alive physically, emotionally, and mentally by a virus. Pain? How about what Mother was going through? Mary Helen shook her head ruefully at her own negligence and thought the two saddest words in the English language—*too late*. Shame hung heavy, a mantle on her shoulders.

She couldn't allow Emory to wither on the vine. He'd quit his job long ago. Mary Helen honestly had no idea how he was supporting himself, what he was doing for food, for friends, how he kept up with utilities and rent.

But those weren't the things that bothered her most, the things that kept her up at night. Worries about practical matters weren't what caused her to weep into her pillow in those long hours between midnight and dawn, when Liz would waken and spoon with her, trying to calm her despair.

The thing that really plagued her was the simple fact she knew her brother was crazy. He'd been for a long time, and Mary Helen had watched his mental illness grow with annoyance, rather than concern. Again—a great wave of guilt and shame rose up. Was there something she could have done that might have prevented him from tumbling into the abyss she was certain he now occupied? Maybe not. But the fact she had done absolutely nothing to try to help weighed on her, made her feel unworthy of life itself.

Only a couple days ago, she'd been to the apartment and found Emory gone. Who knew where? Certainly not to a job! But she'd used the time alone to snoop. She was both glad and horrified she did. What she'd discovered made her tremble, sick to her stomach.

Because what she'd found was a nightmare.

The letters from Jeffrey Dahmer and the bulletin board of newspaper clippings about him—it was nuts and macabre, going beyond what might be considered a normal fascination with true crime or popular culture. It seemed as though Emory had collected every single bit of news published about the man locally and was, in a bizarre way, memorializing the twisted tale of the cannibal killer. The bulletin board was a shrine. It made her heart ache in a literal way—a tightness she could feel.

And the letters? She'd sat on the floor and read them all with growing horror. But when it dawned on her why they looked so familiar—that's when the tears began, and she choked back sobs.

They were all in Emory's handwriting.

It made her gasp to think he was so delusional that he was writing these letters to himself. Did he actually believe the infamous killer was his friend, regularly writing from prison?

How sad and bizarre was that?

My brother has Jeffrey Dahmer for an imaginary playmate.

God! Emory's so lonely. I knew that. I knew it for years. To think his loneliness has now morphed into something so, so—what? Pathetic? Sad? Terrifying? Mary Helen pondered for a long time before cluing Liz in on what she'd discovered that afternoon a couple of days ago. The admission wasn't easy for Mary Helen to make— in a way she knew was illogical and unfair, she felt tainted by association anyway.

Liz. She'd been so supportive, so loving, unlike anyone Mary Helen had ever known, save for her own sainted mother when she had been well, vibrant, and capable of love. Mary Helen had resisted Liz for a long time because she was twenty years older, because she wasn't nearly as pretty as some of the other women she'd met at the Paris dance bar on Montrose Avenue. Hell, Liz had never even been to the dance club. She'd said she was too old for the place and besides, there were too many lipstick lesbians there for her taste.

Mary Helen had met Liz at the grocery store, of all places. The Dominick's on Broadway. They'd fought over the last package of Oreos in the shelf, for Christ's sake. Their beginning was so disgustingly cute Mary Helen was embarrassed. She'd told people they'd met at The Closet, a bar farther south on Broadway.

But Liz had kept after Mary Helen even though Mary Helen had been reluctant to even go on a single date with her. She'd told her to her face she was too old, too butch, too in the camp of joints like the Mountain Moving Coffeehouse for Womyn and Children, a place where a man needed special dispensation to simply get in the door. Separatist lesbian, that's what Mary Helen had called her.

Until she got to know her...

Thank God, Liz had been persistent. Thank God, she saw something in Mary Helen that even Mary Helen herself hadn't seen.

"You're a good person," Liz had said once, early on. "You can hide behind the spiky punk hair, the makeup, patchouli, and a cloud of cigarette smoke, but I see you for the woman you really are. You don't want to admit it, honey, but you're a gal with heart."

Mary Helen, at first, hated Liz for her insight, thinking she could never live up to what this woman thought of her.

But gradually, she began letting Liz in because she was someone who actually *saw* Mary Helen, not as a body to be exploited, as so many of her one-night stands did, but as a person of genuine value and character.

And it was this person who'd responded when Liz told her, only last night, "You need to get up to Edgewater and make sure Emory's okay. Or not. Well, we both know he isn't. You're his only family, hon. It falls on you to take care of him. Do that and maybe your tears at night will start to dry up. Because by taking care of someone you love, you take care of yourself too. In a way, you could even say it's selfish. But I've learned that our only real happiness comes from reaching out toward others."

Once upon a time, Mary Helen would have rolled her eyes at the speech, would have snickered at the earnest words.

But not anymore.

In the recent past, Mary Helen had begun seeing herself through Liz's eyes—with love. And her physical self then morphed. Gone was the heavy mascara and other war-paint-like trappings she hid behind. She'd begun to grow her hair out, allowing it to return to its natural reddish brown. It now hung in curls just above her shoulders. The spikes and peroxide were gone. Once upon a time, she'd thought her outrageous clothes, makeup, and hair were all designed to call attention to herself; now she realized they were a big shield, something to hide behind, a potion for invisibility.

A fat raindrop fell all by itself and splatted on Mary Helen's forehead, interrupting her reverie. The droplet reminded her she wasn't here to ruminate or to glory in how she'd changed for the better.

She was here for her brother.

The raindrop was quickly followed by another and then another—faster, faster. Suddenly, with the flourishes of a flash of lightning and a deafening crack of thunder, the late afternoon skies opened and emptied a torrent of water.

Mary Helen dashed under the awning that led to her old building's front door. She paused, already soaked to the skin through her jeans, black T-shirt, and denim jacket, staring out at the street, which had become a watercolor blur, an obscured vision in gray. She panted even though she'd only run a few steps.

The drumming of the rain on the awning above her head was loud, but also a comfort. She thought she could easily stand here throughout the storm, listening to its percussive and calming beats.

She was delaying the inevitable because she was dreading it. Confronting Emory had seemed like a good idea when she set off from hers and Liz's apartment a little more than an hour ago. Now it seemed like more of a challenge than she needed to take on.

I mean, come on, I'm coping with Mother's death too. I'm dealing with a new relationship and making it work. I'm trying to sort out my own issues, some possibly self-destructive, and need time and comfort to find my own way in the world.

Liz's voice chided her, "The only way to feel whole, to feel happy, is by being selfless and helping. You do need to take care of yourself first, true, and put your oxygen mask on before anyone else. But once that's in place, sweetie, your brother needs you, whether he knows it or not."

Mary Helen reached into her damp front pocket, glad she'd held on to the keys to the building. She wrestled them out and went inside.

At her old front door, she paused, deciding against using her key and simply barging in, justified as she might feel. Even though she *could* do that, she didn't think it was right, even under these bizarre circumstances. She'd moved out. She had no right, not anymore.

So she raised her hand and, for the first time in her life, knocked on that familiar front door. She inclined her head toward the scarred wood, listening. It was dead quiet in the apartment and she wondered if Emory was even here. The only sound was the rain still pouring down outside. The darkness filtering in through the window at the end of the hall made it seem later than it was, more like full-on night. And the sconces along the wallpapered corridor seemed unnaturally bright, almost eerie.

Mary Helen felt a chill.

An entirely illogical sense of foreboding made her want to turn and run—back to Liz, back to the safety of their cluttered little lair, back to where the world was normal.

You've come this far. He needs you.

She knocked again, harder and longer this time.

And waited.

She had a sudden vision of her brother inside, scrambling to hide grisly artifacts—a black plastic skull, a rubber hand, bloody stumps. More letters from his hero...

Or worse.

I don't have a good feeling about this. Maybe I could go home and come back with Liz? She's more level-headed. She'll help me. This was a fool's errand.

She'd turned away from the door, comforted by this new plan. She was sorry she'd wasted her time on this one. She was already feeling a sense of relief as she imagined coming back later tonight with Liz when she heard the door creak open behind her.

Emory peered out at her from the crack he'd made by opening the door maybe a foot at most. "Mary Helen? What are you doing here?"

Mary Helen turned. It was hard to see Emory. For one, he'd only opened the door a crack, and for another, he was backlit by the overhead light in the apartment behind him. Mary Helen moved toward the door and, as she neared her brother, gently placed a hand on his chest to maneuver him out of the way as she stepped inside.

She still had trouble believing the apartment was Spartan clean. Every surface practically sparkled. There was not one throw pillow, dish, picture frame, or knickknack out of place. The air smelled of Lysol and Murphy's Oil Soap.

"Wow," was all she could manage.

Emory said nothing in response. She looked him up and down, shocked at the difference in him. "What did you do to yourself?" she whispered. "What happened to this place?" She was mystified. Her brother looked like a skinhead, a thug, really, but one with really, really good personal hygiene. He seemed bigger, stronger than she remembered, as if he'd grown a couple inches since the last time she saw him.

Emory didn't say anything for a long time; then he said, "I'm just taking care of myself. Keeping everything clean. A clean body, a clean home—a clean mind." He smiled, but the expression didn't travel upward to his eyes, which were dead. Mary Helen shivered.

Usually, she thought, keeping a tidy home and taking care of one's own self would be signs of stability and mental health.

But not in this case. There was something sterile and creepy about the way the apartment had changed, about how her brother had changed. There was an element of fanaticism to it that broke her heart.

They stood for a while in silence near the front door. Mary Helen was uncertain what she should do next. She turned and peered out at the dim light beyond the rain-smeared windows. Now that she was here, she was clueless as to what she should do.

Should she try to get Emory to come with her? Of course, that was her ultimate goal—to get him home, her home, and to see how she might help him. But how to accomplish that? *I can't just tell him I think he's off his rocker, not even in the kindest way. I can't simply drag his ass out of here, much as I'd like to.*

"Emory. Can we just sit down and talk for a bit? I feel like we don't know each other anymore. I know some of that's my fault—" She broke off midsentence when she noticed another aspect to his demeanor—he was nervous, shifting his gaze around the room, anywhere but on Mary Helen's face, where he'd have to meet her gaze directly.

He kept glancing toward Mother's old room.

She cocked her head and blurted, "Are you hiding something?" She said the words simultaneously with the thought occurring to her.

He laughed, and it was weird—high-pitched, abnormal. She swallowed to try to produce some saliva. *I wish I could leave! Liz, I want to come home!*

"What would I be hiding?"

They still stood near the front door. Mary Helen walked to the couch, sat, hoping Emory would join her. He moved to the other side of the room, though, away from the front door and closer to the hallway that led to the master bedroom, Mother's old room. He looked over his shoulder, fast, and then back at her. The color in his cheeks was high.

Suspicious.

"What's going on, Emory?"

"I don't know what you're talking about."

"You do." She patted the cushion next to her. "Come sit down, okay? I just want to talk to you, man."

But before he could respond in any way, by speaking or moving, a sound caused her to stiffen—a loud bang and then a muffled cry.

The noises issued from Mother's old room.

Mary Helen leaped to her feet, eyeing her brother with new and more profound worry. "What's going on?" she repeated. "Is there someone here?"

A muffled scream made the fine hairs on her neck rise.

Mary Helen stood, wary. Her hands trembled. Her heart began to pound and her breath to quicken. She took a couple of steps toward the sound, which had now morphed into a thumping as though someone were banging something on the floor over and over again. This noise was punctuated every couple of seconds by another garbled scream.

"You need to go." Emory wrung his hands, moving near her.

And suddenly, Mary Helen was terrified of her brother, chilled at his nearness. The fight or flight instinct rose up and—coward that she cursed herself for—the flight aspect of the equation was winning out.

She stopped and noticed the wildness in his eyes, the high color in his cheeks, and the line of sweat forming in beads along his hairline.

"I'm not going," Mary Helen insisted with every ounce of courage she possessed. She knew she wanted nothing more than to obey her brother, get out of this suffocating nightmare. "I need to know what's going on here."

She drew in a breath, reaching deep within herself for courage she wasn't sure was there, and forced herself to walk to Mother's old room.

"Don't go in there!" Emory cried, yet he made no move to stop her. She expected his hands, yanking her back, strong-arming her out the front door.

But Emory didn't touch her.

A shiver ran up and down her spine.

All she could do right now was act even if it went against every self-protective instinct. Without hesitation, she opened her mother's bedroom door and stepped inside.

The grunting, muffled cries, and pounding were much louder here.

They came from the closet.

"Oh God, Emory, what have you done?"

I can't. I don't wanna. That door stays shut. Run, run, run!

She found it curious that Emory didn't answer her question. She could sense him behind her, watching, waiting.

"This has to end here, little brother. Now," she said, her voice barely above a choked whisper. *Oh God, what has he done? What am I going to see?*

Mary Helen flung open the closet door. She stuffed a fist in her mouth at what awaited her—a young man, naked, bound, duct tape over his mouth, pale eyes alive with terror. Those eyes begged her for help.

"Oh no! No. This isn't happening."

Mary Helen rushed into the closet, dropping to her knees to free the man, who suddenly went still, eyes even wider with terror as he gazed over her shoulder.

She turned to see what had frightened him even more than this twisted nightmare where he took center stage.

And her brother, the milquetoast, the weakling, the butt of her pity and scorn, stood above her, enraged, a heavy ceramic gargoyle Mother had once made, ready to bring it down on Mary Helen's skull.

She raised a hand and whimpered, too scared to think.

Chapter Twenty

She can't. She's going to ruin everything. This simply cannot happen. This is my house. My man.

Emory brought the gargoyle up high, intent on smashing it down on Mary Helen's skull. The thought of doing so made him sick, but the alternative was worse. She'd free Tyler. They'd go to the police. Just as with Dahmer, they'd never understand why he was keeping Tyler here. They'd say he was holding him prisoner, that he'd kidnapped him.

No one but Dahmer could *get* what he was doing—simply trying to ensure Tyler, whom he knew cared deeply for him, to stay.

That's all—just stay with him, even if it was only for a little bit longer. Emory realized it was all he'd ever wanted—despite the hatred for himself that had hardened his own heart—a man to call his own.

Yes, he knew it was a strange way to go about things, but it was the end result that mattered, wasn't it?

Mary Helen's head was before him, her dun-colored hair, now grown out, no longer colored or spiky, a target. He imagined, for a moment, the skull opening, the blood that would pour out, perhaps even a glimpse of the gray matter that was her brain. In his mind's eye, he watched her crumple to the floor, the whoosh of air, perhaps final, coming out. He saw the pool of blood widening beneath her head.

He started to bring the gargoyle down—swiftly and hard—when she turned to look up at him, eyes wide, mouth open in a little circle of horror and fear. Speechless. Terrified. Hurt.

He almost couldn't halt the downward momentum, so set was his body on completing the motion that could well end in his sister's death.

My own sister.

In an instant, like the reel of his own life that's supposed to unspool in the mind's eye in the moment before death, he saw scenes with Mary Helen and him growing up. He saw himself walking her in the burnt-orange-and-yellow floral-patterned stroller through the neighborhood. The boys would laugh, point, and snicker, but Emory, red-faced, tried not to care. He loved the little girl with all his heart. It was Emory and Mary Helen against the world. There they were at a carnival in a church parking lot on Sheridan Road, Emory's arm wrapped protectively around his little sister as they rose high into the night sky on the Ferris wheel. They were surrounded by neon and the smells of cotton candy, popcorn, and fried food and the screams and laughter of other carnival-goers. Here they were, playing a game called "Daddy and Geraldine." Emory would kneel on the hardwood floor of the living room, hold out his arms and cry, "Geraldine!" and Mary Helen would answer back, "Daddy!" and run into his waiting arms.

"Stop, Emory. Stop." Mary Helen was almost on her back on the floor next to Tyler, her trembling palms up and extended toward him. Her eyes were bright with fear and something else—the sting of betrayal maybe?

She scooted back, and as she did, Emory lowered the gargoyle to his side.

Nearly breathless, Mary Helen asked, "Were you—" She swallowed hard, groping for words. "Were you gonna hit me with that?" Her eyes, wide, welled with tears. "Were you gonna try to kill me?" Her eyes twisted shut for a moment as though her pain was too great to endure.

Maybe it was.

And like the air going out of a balloon, Emory's rage left him, usurped by shame.

He dropped to the floor, letting go of the heavy art object, where it left a dent and scuff in the wood. He put hands over his face and, beneath his palms, let out an unearthly scream. It almost sounded as though it came from someone else—Mother, perhaps, expressing her anguish at seeing her children like this, or a wounded animal.

When the scream ended, he lowered his hands and stared at the two of them, cowering, lost-for-words, staring back. Both of them were trembling. In their eyes and through their eyes, he witnessed himself.

And he understood their terror and upset.

It's because of you. They're scared to death of you. Can you blame them?

"Were you, Emory? Would you hurt me? Your little sister?"

All Emory could do was move toward his flinching sister and gather her up in his arms. He began to sob as he whispered into her hair, "No, no, honey. I could never hurt you. I was crazy there for just a moment. I wish I could say I don't know what came over me, but I do." He looked away, glancing over at Tyler, who eyed him with revulsion and horror.

Tyler will never be mine.

"You're my sister. I couldn't, wouldn't, hurt you. It was a close call. Forgive me, okay?"

Mary Helen wriggled free from his embrace, which he realized was probably too tight, too painful. She stood on shaking legs, grabbing onto the bar for hanging clothes for support. She took a few deep, quivering breaths. Her face was white, slicked with a thin sheen of sweat. At last, she turned, leaving him alone on the floor with Tyler.

He listened without moving as her rapid footfalls propelled her to the front door—and then the door opening and, after a beat, closing softly.

He looked down at Tyler. "I wouldn't have done it. I wouldn't," he said. "You could see that, right?"

If Tyler had an opinion, he wasn't giving it. He couldn't if he wanted to, anyway, with his mouth taped shut.

Emory breathed in deeply and began loosening the bonds that held Tyler and pulling the duct tape off his mouth gently.

"I'm so sorry for this," Emory said, over and over, almost a litany. "I just wanted us to be together. My intentions were good, Ty. I like you."

Tyler, even with his mouth untaped, said nothing, only eyed Emory with the kind of look one might reserve for a murderer or a psychopath, cunningly revealing himself from the shadows in some lonely and deserted place. His face and his body language agreed—he simply wanted to escape this nightmare Emory had cast him in against his will.

At last, gasping and with great effort, Tyler pulled himself to his feet. He paused for a moment and then asked, "Where are my clothes?"

"In my bedroom."

Tyler left the closet.

Emory found him after a few moments, getting dressed in Emory's own bedroom. He was having trouble putting things on because his hands shook so badly. "Let me help you." Emory reached out a hand.

And Tyler pulled away, moving out of reach.

"Stay. I can explain. Just let me talk to you."

Dressed, Tyler turned and began to move from the room to the front door.

"You're not going to the police, are you? You know I did this because I was lonely, because I wanted you in my life."

Tyler opened the front door and stood framed in the doorway for a moment. He shook his head. Emory was surprised to see the tiniest of smiles flicker across Tyler's handsome face. Surprised and hopeful.

But then he said, "Dude, you're nuts."

And just like that, he was gone.

Emory moved to the couch, thinking his entire world had just ended with the soft click of the front door closing.

He swiveled, getting himself up on his knees on the couch so he could watch Tyler from the window. He dared not hope he'd return, and he was right. Tyler walked quickly away never once looking back until he vanished from view around the corner at Granville.

Emory turned back once more, flopping almost supine on the couch, breathing hard. His stomach roiled. He was on the verge of tears.

He wished he would vomit.

He wished he would sob.

But his body offered him no succor.

I've ruined everything. I've driven away the very, very few connections I had to the human race. I'm lost! Lost!

Briefly, he considered writing to Dahmer, but cast aside the idea almost immediately. Here in the harsh glare of the sun coming in through the windows, he knew at last what an empty gesture that would be.

In his mind's eye, he watched himself all those many, many times first writing to Dahmer and then, after a bit, penning his reply, not even bothering to vary the handwriting. He'd never seen himself with such clarity before. Somehow, a place in his brain had misfired and allowed him to actually believe the crazed cannibal serial killer, the man from Milwaukee, was actually paying attention to him, writing to him, Emory Hughes.

He let out a short laugh at his own folly, his own capacity for delusion.

And then he was silent—for many hours, breathing slowly as the quality of light in the room went through its many changes—dimming, dimming until at last Emory was alone in the dark, alone in the world too.

And when the light was finally all sucked from the apartment—and his soul—Emory stood and crossed to where he'd assembled the bulletin board of clippings about Dahmer and, below, his ridiculous cache of so-called correspondence.

He gathered all the paper together and carried the stack into the kitchen. He placed them in the sink and opened the drawer next to the gas stove, where they kept a box of wooden matches for the purpose of lighting the stove's pilot light when it went out, as it often did.

He gazed down at the pictures of Dahmer, the news items, and, worst of all, the letters for only a few moments before striking the match head against the red strip on the box's side. He lifted the flame aloft and watched it flicker in the dark room, mesmerized. He let it burn down to just the moment before his fingertips would be scorched and then dropped it onto the paper.

The pile started to blacken, and then the flames rose.

Emory was stunned at how quickly the paper—and his dreams—went from solid and real to black ash in the kitchen sink.

Mundane was the act of running water over the ashes, observing their progress to the drain, which Emory hoped wouldn't clog.

Part Four

November 1994

Chapter Twenty-One

"In those days shall men seek death, and shall not find it; and shall desire to die..."

Tyler put the *Chicago Tribune* from that morning aside because he needed to stop and think. The quote was from Revelations, chapter nine, verse six. The article, about the beating death of serial killer Jeffrey Dahmer, referenced biblical verse because it said that Dahmer, shortly before his killing at the hands of another inmate, had been meeting with a minister. The minister had been Dahmer's only visitor at the Columbia Correctional Institution in Portage, Wisconsin. Revelations was their latest foray into Bible study.

The quote, based on what had happened, seemed *apt*.

"Yeah, I guess so. Apt is a good word." Tyler mumbled to himself. He sat in silence for a long time, long enough for the coffee at his side, once steaming, to go cold.

He too felt chilled.

The article went on to quote the minister, who told the *Tribune* that "Dahmer wanted to die." The minister imagined Dahmer's greatest surprise was that it had taken so long for death to catch up to him in a prison bathroom on a Monday morning.

Tyler imagined waiting and wondering when death would come for a person. What a way to exist—calling that kind of existence "living" was a stretch.

And then his thoughts turned to a face from his past...

It had been years since Tyler had even laid eyes on Emory Hughes. Tyler believed he'd escaped from the man's insane clutches in both literal and figurative terms. But this morning's news had reawakened old ties. Tyler was under the mistaken impression he'd wiped those ties from his memory since that long-ago day when Emory had drugged and imprisoned him in his Kenmore Avenue apartment.

Other than Emory's sister, Mary Helen, Tyler assumed no one knew about his harrowing confinement and what might have happened if she hadn't dropped by and heard his struggles. She'd rescued him and, in the process, had been nearly killed herself.

The whole short period seemed now like a nightmare, surreal, something that maybe he'd read about in a newspaper account, rather than a chapter from his own life.

Tyler could never bring himself to contact the police although he knew he should have done so. It was the sane, rational move. But going through such channels would have made things *real*, and Tyler didn't know if he could bear the crushing weight of the nightmare crime that had been his to bear.

Tyler couldn't even tell the man who would become his partner, Cole Hardwick, about what had happened during those fateful days. Cole had pressed and pressed shortly after Tyler's release because he'd worried so much when Tyler had turned up missing, but Tyler had put him off with vague excuses—a family emergency morphed into time alone to sort his thoughts. Cole had never believed him, not really. But Tyler had been aware Cole could also see the grief talking about his own absence caused, and Cole had kindly left him alone, perhaps waiting until Tyler was ready to tell him the full story.

He still wasn't ready. He didn't know if he'd ever be.

He'd never told his family. They certainly would have insisted on police interference. They would have wanted vengeance.

Tyler simply couldn't do that to Emory. He pitied him way more than he hated him and knew he acted out of delusion and very, very weirdly, love for Tyler.

And the result? Emory hadn't been arrested, as far as Tyler knew. He could even be walking around today, a free man. A twinge of guilt went through him as his conscience reminded him that Emory could have done to some other hapless young man what had been done to Tyler.

Yet, Tyler didn't think so.

With his thwarted attempt on his sister's life, Emory's steam went out of him. It was as though a switch had been flipped—it happened that fast. There was a kind of reckoning, remorse. Tyler could see it in Emory's eyes, even though it didn't stop him from getting away from the man as fast as he could.

He'd thrown up at the corner of Kenmore and Granville that day, on and on until he was heaving, and nothing more came out of his mouth other than yellow bile and strands of spit. Typical of Chicago, none of the passersby stopped to ask if he'd needed help.

He'd tried, from that day on, to get on with his life as though nothing had happened, as though he hadn't been cast in the victim role in one of those horror movies that gets its value not from supernatural monsters, but from the terrors that walk on two legs in and out of our everyday lives—movies like *Silence of the Lambs*, *The Texas Chainsaw Massacre*, *Henry: Portrait of a Serial Killer*, and, of course, *Psycho*. Tyler had once enjoyed horror movies, got a little kick from them and had even enjoyed them with Emory himself.

But no more. These days, Tyler's speed, when it came to cinema, was more for romantic comedies, family dramas, and what Cole referred to as "chick flicks."

He didn't care. Cole didn't know about the nightmares that had never completely gone away, that horror of waking up screaming and having to reassure himself he was okay, that it was only a dream. Only a dream seemed a weak excuse—when the terror that visited him at night, in his slumber, was something monstrous.

After a while, Tyler drew in a deep breath, got up to get himself some hot coffee, and sat back down with his newspaper. He was glad Cole was at work because news of Dahmer's passing reignited his trauma and fear.

And pity.

Where was Emory now?

He read on and learned how Dahmer had been beaten to death by another inmate. The suspect was a high school dropout who was also serving a life sentence at the prison for the execution-style slaying of a Wisconsin Conservation Corps crew chief. The suspect had been laid off from the Corps' carpentry training program.

One sentence from the article caused the coffee to roil sickly in Tyler's gut.

"The way Dahmer died has renewed the lurid attention that ensures he will continue to live, at least for a while, in notoriety."

Did Emory continue to live? In obscurity?

Where was he now?

Tyler learned this was the second attempt on Dahmer's life in fewer than five months.

Did Emory still believe Dahmer had written to him? That he was his friend—a confidante?

What made Tyler finally stand and take the newspaper outside, where he could deposit it in the dumpster behind his building in the Rogers Park neighborhood, was the report that Dahmer had been discovered on "the floor of the staff bathroom next to the gym at 8:10 a.m., unresponsive and bleeding from massive head wounds. A bloody broom handle lay nearby."

The reference to the massive head wounds caused a memory, like some Technicolor nightmare to arise—that of Emory about to swing a heavy gargoyle sculpture down on his sister's head.

As he let the paper flutter onto the plastic trash bags, he saw that Dahmer had died at a hospital in Portage. Its name? Divine Savior.

*

It was getting close to evening when Tyler finally returned home, the horizon behind him a mix of navy, purple, lavender, and tangerine. The air had a snap to it. A cold front was moving in from the north. The smell of snow was in the air.

Soon, winter would be upon them, the edge of the lake fringed with ice. The darkness would seem endless, the bitter winds and the snow a bad dream from which there was no escape—spring a bitter promise on the horizon, disbelieved.

Tyler entered the small lobby of the two-flat apartment building he shared with Cole. The owners, an older gay couple he and Cole referred to Lucy and Ethel when they were out of earshot, lived on the first floor and had converted the basement into a suite with a bedroom, bathroom, and office; the first floor was their living area.

They were good landlords, minded their own business, but they were characters, to be sure. One had a doll fixation and collected Barbies and the other never left the house, staying inside and reading books by people like Jane Austen and Emily Bronte.

The mailbox was empty, and Tyler concluded that meant Cole was home. He unlocked the door to the staircase that led up to their apartment and trudged wearily up the stairs.

It was time.

If he couldn't share what Emory had done to him with Cole, then what *was* their relationship, really? The period Tyler was confined, bound and naked, on that closet floor were the worst hours of his young life. He really believed he might die.

He now knew he needed to unburden that darkness with the man he loved.

Cole was in the kitchen, humming tunelessly. Their biggest pot was on one burner and a smaller saucepan on the other. Cole was in the pantry. When he came out, he smiled at Tyler as though nothing was wrong.

Why would he believe anything was wrong?

Even with Dahmer's murder splashed luridly all over the news, what difference did it make to them, a young gay couple in Chicago?

It makes all the difference.

"Hey," Cole said, drawing near and giving Tyler a quick peck. "I'm just getting started on dinner. I wondered where you were. Out for a walk? I'm keeping it simple tonight, just some spaghetti and jarred sauce. And I can whip up a salad. There's still some romaine in the fridge and we have those cherry tomatoes—"

Tyler put a hand on his chest to stop the blather. "Please," he whimpered. Suddenly, he felt very close to tears. *There will be time for those later.* "Please," he repeated. "We need to talk."

Cole stepped back as though he had struck him in the chest, rather than just placing his hand there. Cole clutched that same hand now, squeezing it. He cocked his head and asked Tyler, "What is it?"

"Let's go in the living room. Sit. Okay?"

He probably thinks I'm going to break up with him. Isn't that what the other half of a couple always thinks when someone says something about needing to talk?

Cole followed him into their spacious living room. It was full dark outside now, but the yellow/gold light from the streetlamp outside filtered in through the ivy partially covering their bay windows. Tyler plopped down on the forest-green couch they'd found at Howard Brown and put his feet up on the coffee table. He supposed he might appear relaxed, but inside, he was shaking so hard he thought he might implode.

Cole sat near him, worry causing his thick, dark eyebrows to furrow together with concern. "You gonna break up with me?"

A short, near hysterical bark of laughter escaped Tyler's lips because of what he'd thought just a minute before. He closed his eyes for a moment, then looked at the man who'd been beside him for the past couple of years. "Is that what you think? Really?" Tyler didn't wait for an answer but shook his head. "There's something I need to tell you about."

Cole sat back a little more, now that he knew he wasn't being dumped, and settled into the couch. "Everything okay? You're okay, right?"

Tyler smiled. "Will you just shut up, and let me tell you?"

Cole eyed him but said nothing more.

And Tyler told him—everything. He started with meeting Emory at work, their odd relationship (if it could even be called that), and ended with Tyler's drugging and confinement. At last, he revealed the dumb luck of Emory's sister unwittingly coming to his rescue.

When he was finished, he sat there, breathing a little harder, but relieved to have finally shared his trauma with someone else. It felt like something at last coming to a head and breaking open. He let his head slide onto Cole's shoulder.

They said nothing for the longest time. The little sounds in the apartment rose up—the steam heat coming on, causing the old radiators to clank and moan, the distant roar of the L train over at Western and Lincoln, the footsteps of their landlords below, and dimly, their laughter. Tyler could even hear, if he listened very closely, the wind moving through the naked boughs of the maple tree outside.

After a long time, Cole spoke, "You know, he—that Dahmer guy—was just killed in prison. By another inmate."

Tyler nodded. "I know. It's what brought everything to a head for me again."

They were quiet again for a while, long enough to make Tyler wonder what was going on in his partner's head. He was about to ask, rather than speculate, when Cole spoke.

"It's all so terrible." He drew in a breath, and it came back out, shaky. "This really happened to you? Honey, it makes my heart hurt. It makes me sick."

"I wouldn't joke about a thing like this, Cole."

"No. No, of course you wouldn't. Part of me wishes you *were*, sweetheart. Because then it wouldn't be true. You wouldn't have lived through that." He turned a bit so he could take Tyler in his arms and hold him. Tyler clung to him, extracting whatever warmth and comfort he could from the hug.

When they pulled away, Cole asked, "You never reported this? You didn't go to the cops?" He shook his head. "Christ, Tyler, what he did was kidnapping. It was assault. Maybe even attempted murder?" He eyed Tyler, and Tyler felt a chill—it was as though Cole had never seen him before.

"I know. I know what I should have done and what I failed to do. Right or wrong, I made my choice, and I don't know that you could ever understand."

Could anyone?

"No. I don't think I can understand." Cole shrugged and stared off into the distance. And then he surprised Tyler by saying, "But I know *you*, and I trust your judgment, even if I personally don't get it. I'm not gonna question why you didn't do this or that, but just try to have faith that you made your choices based on *something*, right? Something that made sense to you."

Tyler was tempted to make a joke about his choice being based on insanity, but that wasn't true. "I could see his pain, you know? I could see how lonely he was. How he had no one, Cole. No one at all. He was this weird guy, and his neediness radiated off him like a smell." Tyler sighed, thinking how inadequate words were. "Here's why I didn't tell on him—I believed back then, shaken up as I was, that he wouldn't do it to someone else. That was first and foremost, you understand. If I thought for a minute he would have, I'd have gone to the authorities. I'm not so selfish that I'd see someone else go through what I went through.

"But here's the thing. I saw the change in him when he was about to slam that gargoyle into Mary Helen's head. I saw the remorse and the pain. It was like he woke up. It's hard to describe, but I think he saw the light, saw that he was sick and that he was going about everything all wrong."

Tyler stood up. "Let *me* finish making dinner, okay? It'll relax me, as much as I can be relaxed."

"There's that shiraz we opened last night."

Tyler smiled. "That'll relax me too."

He turned in the archway separating the living room from the dining room as he headed for the kitchen. "I couldn't tell on him because I felt like it would have been cruel. I couldn't do that to him."

Cole regarded him, and Tyler felt hopeless. Even the most sympathetic human in the world could never comprehend his motivation and could certainly feel no empathy toward him.

But Cole once again surprised him. "And this," he said, "is why I love you."

To staunch the flow of tears, Tyler hurried away, into the kitchen, where he could drink wine, cook, and think about what he should do next—if anything.

Chapter Twenty-Two

Interstate 55 south thrummed beneath their feet, Mary Helen's little red Sentra eating up the gray pavement and leaving its gravelly trail in their wake.

It was a bright morning in early December, and Mary Helen was glad for the shades on her face. They hid the red moistness of her eyes.

She'd been crying since she first heard from her passenger, Tyler Kay, whom she hadn't seen since that fateful day in her mother's closet. He'd called her just a couple of days ago, out of the blue. *But when is anything, really, out of the blue? Liz always says everything happens for a reason, that our lives are unfolding just as they should.* Usually, Mary Helen thought the woman she regarded as her wife now was regurgitating her Science of Mind teachings, but today, on this crisp, cold, sunny morning, she realized there was truth to her pronouncements. *Maybe life isn't so random, after all.*

When she'd picked up the phone the other day, right after hello, a male voice said, "This is Tyler Kay. I don't know if you remember me, but a few years ago, you saved my life."

At the sound of this, Mary Helen's arm jerked in a spasm, so hard the cordless in her hand clattered to the hardwood floor. She picked it up, seriously contemplating simply replacing it in the charging cradle without saying a word.

Of course she remembered him.

The day they'd shared would be forever seared into her memory as though branded on the soft pink tissue of her brain. It was a day she'd forget if she could—yet when she came close to obscuring it, it rose up in a nightmare or an actual memory of turning to see her brother about to bash her head in.

She still couldn't believe it. Any of it. Not the attempt on her life. Not the fact that poor Emory, poor misguided, love-starved and lonely Emory, had followed in a notorious killer's footsteps and had attempted to keep the man he was fixated on a prisoner.

Other than Liz, she'd never shared with anyone what had happened that day.

She assumed those events could be buried below the surface. Never out of reach, but maybe, when she was really lucky, out of mind.

The news of Dahmer's death reignited the terror and the nausea.

Tyler Kay's phone call made it as real as if the bad things had occurred only yesterday.

When she found her voice, she asked how he'd found her.

"You're in the book. MH Hughes. The MH was a giveaway. Women tend to use initials when phones are in their name."

Mary Helen chuckled nervously because that was exactly why she'd listed herself that way. "I think it was the other way around, Mr. Kay. You saved my life."

Tyler didn't respond for a moment. Then he said, "Let's just go with we saved each other."

"And I'm grateful. Grateful we can talk today."

Mary Helen wasn't so sure she was grateful for this last part. *How can I ask him what he wants without being rude?*

It was as though he'd read her mind. "You're probably wondering why I'm calling after all this time."

"Crossed my mind." Mary Helen searched automatically for her cigarettes. She'd quit a long time ago, but this was an occasion when the urge rose up, making her crave one again, for the comfort, for having something to do with her hands.

"I suppose you saw the news about Jeffrey Dahmer."

Just the mention of Dahmer's name made the fine hair on the back of her neck rise. She shivered. "Yeah, I saw something about it on the news. Another inmate, right?"

"Yeah."

I'm still wondering why you called me.

"It got me thinking. Thinking about your brother—and wondering." Tyler drew in a shaky breath, and Mary Helen wondered if he was about to cry. *Don't cry. I can't handle that. I'll hang up.*

Mercifully, he must have pulled himself together because when he spoke again, he sounded a bit more composed. "Wondering what's up with Emory, if he's okay." He paused for a long moment. "See, despite everything that happened, I really cared about your brother. In spite of it all, I don't hate him or wish bad things on him."

"No one would blame you if you did."

"No one would blame *you*."

"Well, I don't know about that." In her mind's eye, she pictured Liz, reminded herself how forgiving she was, how she'd held the key to Mary Helen's relationship with

Emory and how that key was one simple word—forgiveness. "How can I ever forgive him?" Mary Helen had cried one of those long, dark nights when she'd woken, screaming. "He was gonna kill me."

And Liz told her that forgiveness was not an act that was for Mary Helen's brother, but for Mary Helen herself. "You'll never feel any kind of peace until you can forgive. This isn't for *him*, baby doll, it's for *you*."

How did Mary Helen get so lucky to have someone like Liz in her life?

Tyler interrupted the memory with a question. "Is he? Is he okay?"

"Not really," Mary Helen had answered.

And she told him all about Emory, bringing him up to date.

*

And now, they rode in companionable silence south, away from Chicago and toward the Morton Psychiatric Hospital and Resident Inpatient facility, across the Illinois River from Peoria.

As they drew closer to the institution, Tyler asked her for the second time, "How is he? What should I expect?"

Mary Helen felt like blurting "Expect the unexpected!" And then laughing uncontrollably, hysterically, as though she was the one who should be in an institution and not her brother. She stared out the window at the bland, flat landscape going by for a moment before responding. The sky was dirty gray, the sides of the road lined with mounds of blackened and graying snow and mud. She sighed. "He's been at Morton since that day it all went down—you know the day." Mary Helen regarded Tyler out of the corner of her eye, but he stared out the window. She could get no gauge. "After we both left him there, I had to go back. I'm his fucking sister, after all. And you know as well as I do that he had no one, not back then and not now either." The thought of this state of protracted aloneness caused her heart to seize up a bit and a lump the size of a tangerine to form in her throat. She sniffed. "I came back after dark and let myself in."

She turned off the main road to head up the long drive to the institution's fieldstone façade. It looked almost gothic—and foreboding. But at least her brother was safe there. *It doesn't really matter where he is. He's in a cocoon of his own making. He's trapped, or staying, in his own head.*

"He was still in the closet." As she spoke, she realized her voice came out more and more monotone, as though it were robbed of emotion, even though what was going on inside was the opposite. Her lips turned up in a half-hearted grin. "And I don't mean that metaphorically. He was *literally* still in the closet, in the dark. When I came upon him, he was simply laying on the floor, in a fetal position, rocking himself.

"He wouldn't speak. Hell, he wouldn't even look at me. That's when I made the call and had him taken to the hospital where he was admitted for a psych evaluation. It didn't take them long to realize he needed much more treatment than a simple overnight stay might provide." She let some air rush out of her and wished once more for the cigarettes she once smoked.

"So he's been at this place ever since?"

Mary Helen nodded. "It's not the best solution, but it's the best we can do. He can't be on his own."

"Does he talk about what happened?"

"Sweetie, he doesn't talk about *anything*. That's what I'm trying to tell you. He's spoken hardly a word since that day we saved each other. He sits and stares out the window. He takes care of himself in the sense that he bathes, eats, watches TV. He's like a zombie."

"So, if he watches TV, then he must know that Dahmer was killed."

"Yes. Unfortunately. One of his caretakers, a nice young man named Dwight, called me to tell me they tried to keep the news from him, but how can you keep national headlines away from someone even if they're institutionalized? Dwight said Emory's been agitated ever since learning that Dahmer was dead—sinking deeper into his own personal darkness."

"What does that even mean?"

"It means that what I said a minute ago, about him taking care of himself, is no longer true. He hasn't showered in a couple of days. He won't eat. He stays in his room and refuses to come out to the common area, something he didn't do before."

Mary Helen was quiet for a long time and so was Tyler. They drove up to the facility and parked in a visitor's space.

When they got out, she looked up at the institution, its gray façade against a brooding sky full of bruised clouds. A chill wind blew out of the north, causing her to cross her arms over her chest. Would it snow today? And if it did, would they get back to Chicago in time to beat it or have to fight their way through a blizzard? She could smell snow in the future.

She glanced over at Tyler. "Are you ready?"

Tyler was pale. "I don't know how to answer that."

Mary Helen let a grim chuckle escape her. "I don't blame you. But I'm hoping maybe your being here will help settle him." She paused as they walked up the wide walk to the big double oak-framed doors—the main entrance. "Or at least not *unsettle* him more."

"But no pressure," Tyler said, so softly she barely heard him.

"No pressure." Mary Helen opened one of the doors for Tyler and followed him inside.

Chapter Twenty-Three

Emory looked out at the day through the only window in his room—it was little more than a long, vertical slit, cross-hatched wire between its double panes. Outside, blackened fingers, the trees' bare limbs, reached up toward a sky that was a mix of white, gray, and charcoal; clouds lay heavy on the horizon.

Most of the land around the facility was barren, flat— empty fields. This emptiness comforted him in a way, made him feel he was alone in the world. And being alone meant he didn't have to confront the demons inside him, demons that had caused him to hurt others, to think that a cannibal killer was a suitable role model for a young man.

In here, life was easy. One day merged almost imperceptibly into another. Time passed quickly for a place where almost nothing ever happened. He ate the meals that were made for him, even if they were disgusting at worst and bland and flavorless at best. He watched endless hours of TV in the common room (although he hadn't graced the room with his presence since he'd heard about Dahmer's passing). He'd sleep for at least ten hours a night, sometimes more if nightmares didn't trouble him.

He didn't read.

He didn't think about the past.

He didn't wonder about the people he once knew because, save for his sister, that world had forgotten him. He no longer felt a part of the walking mass of contradictions, dashed dreams, and futile hopes he thought of as humanity.

Empty was enough. He could go on like this forever.

He had to admit, though, if only to himself, that news of Dahmer's passing had stung, maybe even shredded a little what remained of his heart. He could imagine Dahmer's fear as that other inmate attacked him, and it made Emory wince, feeling the blows in a kind of psychic communion.

No. Those days were over, he told himself. *Those days are the ones that landed me here. There's no connection between me and him. There's no connection at all.*

There never was.

His head snapped up as footfalls and subdued voices on the tiled floor of the corridor outside his room sounded. He recognized Mary Helen's voice, but not the male one. He turned away from the window and faced the door. *What do I need to get through now?*

Keys jingled and then an attendant pulled the metal door open.

Mary Helen came into view first. He was always surprised when he saw her, how dowdy and matronly she'd become in just a few years. Still, she was always a welcome sight, one that reminded him there was at least one soul in the world who still cared.

And then, behind her, there he was.

Emory sucked in a breath.

Tyler. What are you doing here? Have you come at last to confront me? To harm me? To kill me? I can't say that I would blame you, not after the way I treated you.

"How's tricks, brother?" Mary Helen smiled as she came into the room. She stopped to pull the thin quilt on his bed up over the sweat-soiled sheets. She lifted his pillow to fluff it and then replaced it on the bed. "I brought you a visitor."

It had been so long since he'd uttered a single word that he was surprised something would emerge from his lips at all. "I see that." *My voice sounds like an old man's. A croak.*

Mary Helen crossed the room a little farther and glanced out the window for a moment. She turned back to say, "It's started snowing. And it's coming down hard. Sad to say we should make this quick. Who knows what 55 will be like in an hour." Her gaze moved to Tyler, who nodded.

Tyler hadn't changed much. His hair had grown out a bit, and he'd gained a few pounds, which he needed to do. He looked more like a grown man and less like a boy just entering adulthood. Emory swallowed hard.

I still love you. The thought emerged out of nowhere, or maybe, more apt, it emerged out of the ether of who Emory used to be.

Mary Helen looked at Emory, then at Tyler, back again. And Emory could see the decision written on her face.

"Why don't I go get us some coffee? Let you two boys get reacquainted." She smiled as though bestowing a gift. She asked Tyler, "Would that be okay?"

Tyler, to his credit, had to think about the question for a moment. Emory supposed, had the tables been turned, he would have to ponder as well. Hell, he'd probably run for the hills.

But Tyler simply said, "It's okay." He sat on the edge of Emory's bed and watched Mary Helen leave the room.

If she was surprised at Emory's speaking, she didn't show it.

After she was gone, Tyler and Emory simply regarded each other for the longest time. Emory had to turn away once he felt Tyler's gaze was too acute, too penetrating. Outside, the sky had grown even darker, and the snow swirled down. Under other circumstances, it might have been pretty, but today, the cold it represented seemed as though it had been brought by Tyler himself.

In an absurd twist, Emory realized he was afraid of Tyler.

"How are you, Emory?"

How does one answer that question? Emory didn't have a clue, so he simply pushed out his own question in response. "Why are you here?" He genuinely wanted to know.

Tyler licked his lips, causing Emory to think of a stressed-out dog. Tyler didn't answer right away. But before too long, he spoke. "My first impulse was to say I honestly don't know. But then, before I rushed to blurt that out, that easy answer, I realized I *did* know." Tyler drew in a breath and patted the bed beside him. "Come sit here."

It wasn't a request and Emory did as he was told, sitting a foot or so from Tyler. He resisted the urge to gnaw on a fingernail. It wouldn't have done any good anyway, since all of his nails were bitten to the quick, so badly on some fingers that there was dried blood in his nail beds. He braced himself for the onslaught of words—the pain and the accusations. He deserved it all and more.

But Tyler surprised him.

"I came here because I think you need closure. At first, I was going to say *I* needed it. But I think I found that particular commodity long ago when I forgave you for what you did."

Emory eyed him but said nothing.

"Does that surprise you? That I forgave you?" Tyler shrugged. "It might have surprised *me*—once. But you know what? Forgiveness isn't about absolving someone. No. I read somewhere that it's really about releasing your own pain, being a survivor rather than a victim. I realized, Emory, I could have trapped myself in my victimhood forever if I didn't forgive you."

Tyler sighed and stared out the window for a moment. Emory didn't dare look away, but he wondered what he saw. Snow coming down? Or the inside of Mother's walk-in closet?

"So I did—forgive. And even though it took a long time, it eventually sank in and I was able to move on. I realized that I might never be able to get a grip on why you did what you did. But I *could* understand the motivation for it and could even see myself in *that*.

"When I heard about Dahmer being killed, I immediately thought of you. I wondered if you were okay. I knew that, in some twisted way, he meant something to you. Can I forgive you for that? Yes. Can I understand that?" Tyler shook his head. "No. Never."

Tyler scooted over a bit and leaned into Emory then, so their shoulders touched.

Emory closed his eyes. More than what Tyler had said, more than his presence, this simple touch moved him, made everything that had been dead inside him come back to life, like a downpour on a desert.

Just like that—a single moment, a single touch from another human being saved him.

Gave him something he never thought he'd have—hope.

He'd had an epiphany—for that's what it was—only once. It was when he was in the fevered state where he thought he must kill his own sister. And then the look in her eyes, her terror and disbelief, immediately reeled him back in, causing him not only to draw back the offending weapon, but for shame—a real, human emotion—to rise.

Emory sat with Tyler for a while with their shoulders touching and reveled in it. How long had it been since he'd felt genuine warmth from another human being? It was a gift Emory didn't know if Tyler himself realized he was bestowing.

Gently, Tyler reached out, wrapping an arm around Emory's back and pulling him closer. "I may not understand the fascination with a killer, or those letters you wrote, but I came to grasp one thing—you did what you did not because you hated me or wanted to hurt me, but because you loved me."

"I wanted you to stay." *There. It's really that simple.*

Tyler looked at him and Emory knew he could see the tears standing in his eyes. One rolled down his cheek and then another and another.

Tyler hugged him hard and whispered, "I know. I know."

And then he let go and pulled away. He stood.

Footsteps sounded outside the door and, again, the jingle of keys, and *whoosh*, the door opened, and Mary Helen stood there, a tray of Styrofoam cups in her hand. The smile vanished from her face as she regarded them, looking from one, sitting and in tears, to the other, standing near a window where outside all was white.

"Everything okay?"

Tyler moved toward her. "Everything's okay." He turned to smile at Emory. "Right?"

And Emory nodded. Sadness, grief even, moved through him. "Everything is okay." He paused, feeling like he might be frozen in this moment forever. And then he realized he was alive and that he could move.

He got up. "Thanks." He lifted a cup of coffee from the tray and took a cautious sip. It burned going down, and Emory imagined it dissolving the lump in his throat.

"You guys should drink yours in the car." Emory glanced out the window. "It's really coming down. Fast and hard." He sat at his desk chair and set his coffee on the desk. He drew in a deep breath.

"And I know Tyler can't stay."

About the Author

Real Men. True Love.

Rick R. Reed is an award-winning and bestselling author of more than fifty works of published fiction. He is a Lambda Literary Award finalist. *Entertainment Weekly* has described his work as "heartrending and sensitive." *Lambda Literary* has called him: "A writer that doesn't disappoint..." Rick lives in Palm Springs, CA, with his husband, Bruce, and their fierce Chihuahua/Shiba Inu mix, Kodi.

Email: rickrreedbooks@gmail.com

Facebook: www.facebook.com/rickrreedbooks

Twitter: @rickrreed

Website: www.rickrreedreality.blogspot.com

Other NineStar books by this author

Unraveling
Sky Full of Mysteries
The Perils of Intimacy
IM
Chaser
Raining Men
Blue Umbrella Sky
Third Eye

Legally Wed
Hungry for Love
Big Love
A Face without a Heart
Bigger Love
Torn
The Secrets We Keep

Also Available from Rick R. Reed

IM

One by one, he's killing them. Lurking in the digital underworld of Men4HookUpNow.com, he lures, seduces, charms, reaching out through instant messages to the unwary. They invite him over. He's just another trick. Harmless. They're dead wrong.

When the first bloody body surfaces, openly gay Chicago Police Department detective Ed Comparetto is called in to investigate. Sickened by the butchered mess of one of his brothers left on display in a bathtub, he seeks relief outside where the young man who discovered the body waits to tell him the story of how he found his friend. But who is this witness...and did he play a bigger part in the murder than he's letting on?

Comparetto is on a journey to discover the truth, a truth that he needs to discover before he loses his career, his boyfriend, his sanity...his life. Because in this killer's world, IM doesn't stand for instant message...it stands for instant murder.

Third Eye

Who knew that a summer thunderstorm and a lost little boy would conspire to change single dad Cayce D'Amico's life in an instant? With Luke missing, Cayce ventures into the woods near their house to find his son, only to have lightning strike a tree near him, sending a branch down on his head. When he awakens the next day in the hospital, he discovers he has been blessed or cursed—he isn't sure which—with psychic ability. Along with unfathomable glimpses into the lives of those around him, he's getting visions of a missing teenage girl.

When a second girl disappears soon after the first, Cayce realizes his visions are leading him to their grisly fates. Cayce wants to help, but no one believes him. The police are suspicious. The press wants to exploit him. And the girls' parents have mixed feelings about the young man with the "third eye."

Cayce turns to local reporter Dave Newton and, while searching for clues to the string of disappearances and possible murders, a spark ignites between them. Little do they know that nearby, another couple—dark and murderous—are plotting more crimes and wondering how to silence the man who knows too much about them.

A Face without a Heart

A modern-day and thought-provoking retelling of Oscar Wilde's *The Picture of Dorian Gray* that esteemed horror magazine *Fangoria* called "...a book that is brutally honest with its reader and doesn't flinch in the areas where Wilde had to look away.... A rarity: a really well-done update that's as good as its source material."

A beautiful young man bargains his soul away to remain young and handsome forever, while his holographic portrait mirrors his aging and decay and reflects every sin and each nightmarish step deeper into depravity... even cold-blooded murder. Prepare yourself for a compelling tour of the darkest sides of greed, lust, addiction, and violence.

Also Available from NineStar Press

Connect with NineStar Press

www.ninestarpress.com

www.facebook.com/ninestarpress

www.facebook.com/groups/NineStarNiche

www.twitter.com/ninestarpress